SIX OF THE B___

Ray Davey

THE CORRYMEELA PRESS

Six Stories for each of our grandchildren
Andrew, Caitlin, Charlotte, Christopher, Kate, Patrick,
Patrick, Peter and Raymond

This book owes its creation to many people.

*Firstly, to **Alan Evans** for his imagination, expertise and encouragement.*
*To **Ian Barnett** for all he has given in many hours of work and constant support.*
*To **Ann McDonagh** for producing manuscript copies at such short notice.*
*To **Carrie Barkley** and the committee for their help at all times.*
*To **Trevor Williams** for his support and for writing the foreword.*
*To **Chris Curry** for all his drawings and to my wife **Kathleen** for her time, patience*
and skill in deciphering and correcting a very untidy script.

Ray Davey
7th of October 2000

Six of the Best

ISBN: 1 873739 15 X
This Edition Published October 2000 by The Corrymeela Press
8 Upper Crescent, Belfast, Northern Ireland BT7 1NT
Text Copyright © Ray Davey 2000
Drawings © Chris Curry 2000
All proceeds of this book will go to support the work of
The Corrymeela Community

FOREWORD

TO MY GRANDCHILDREN

I have written this book because I believe that one of the most important relationships in life is between young and old and is very often sadly overlooked or indeed forgotten. I write because we, the old, and you, the young really need each other.

For many reasons it has often been a difficult time and the fault has been on both sides. On the one hand young people feel that the old live in a world that is long since dead, are very set in their attitudes and refuse to listen to their point of view. On the other hand old people feel that the young are impatient and don't want to listen but they fail to consider that there many important things that do not change.

My belief is that both these attitudes are not only wrong but very sad and because of them both miss so much. The truth is that we really need each other and when we do listen, talk and relate, we are both vastly enriched and fulfilled.

I am now quite old. I'll not give exact details but some of the following stories will provide plenty of clues! I know very well that I can no longer do many of the things that you can. I have, however, one thing that you do not have and that is a greater experience of life. It is this that I wish to share with you in these stories.

It is important that we really listen to each other. There must be a continual dialogue between us. When we do this, we complement and encourage each other. It must be open and understanding with real give and take.This is the highway to a full and balanced life.

So, for my grandchildren or the casual reader, I hope that some of what I have written might create genuine discussion and dialogue.

Love Grandad

INTRODUCTION

It's a pleasure to have the opportunity to write a few words in 'Six of the Best'.

For me, this book is typical of Ray. The picture of Ray that I carry in my mind is of him sitting alongside a much younger person, with Ray listening intently.

The other day one of the volunteer team at the Corrymeela Centre talked about a meeting they had had with Ray and his wife Kathleen. Ray had told them about the beginnings of Corrymeela in 1965 and its story through the last 35 years. "But the best bit," said this young adult volunteer "was when we just chatted one to one, afterwards. Ray is such an inspiration".

Ray's style of leadership is in giving confidence to others to achieve what they think is impossible. I have heard it said time and time again, of how a young person came to Ray and spilled out their idea of 'what someone should do,' or new way of doing things. Ray would listen and then say, 'I think you are the person who could do that'. And they did.

Ray believes in young people, their imagination and their energy. He believes in the vision of young people, and is willing to take the risk alongside them. Ray knows that some of the most important lessons that Corrymeela has learnt, have come through the mistakes we have made. In his mid eighties, Ray is still young at heart.

The importance of young people to Corrymeela, the youth programmes, the young adult volunteers who are central to the running of the Centre, is the fruit of Ray's ability to inspire the young and give them a place.

From this book it is clear that what we know about how well Ray gets on well with young people at Corrymeela is also true of his family.

A big part of Corrymeela is sharing our story with one another. Ray taught us that a powerful way of building community is to listen to one another's story. Here Ray is again using stories to point to some of the core values that are central to his life.

I know that his grandchildren have enjoyed these stories. I know you will too.

Trevor Williams - Leader of The Corrymeela Community

CONTENTS

DOING THE UNEXPECTED

Dear Andrew, I know you have visited some of the battlefields in France and been deeply impressed, so I thought this story might interest you.

Professor John Barkley in his book "Blackmouth and Dissenter" recounts a wonderful story told by a French Pastor about what happened in his parish in Hunspach in Alsace during the final weeks of the last war. As the German Army was being driven back into Germany, the soldiers had dug trenches in which they had placed mines under the village so that when they were retreating, they could detonate them by remote control. Another nearby village called Inglesheim, had been completely destroyed in this way. But Hunspach had a different story to tell. One Sunday at this terrible time Pastor Fidel asked his congregation to pray for him. Everyone knew why. He was going to slip out of the village and try to contact the German Commander and ask him to spare the village. No one could help him, as he had to do it himself.

One evening at dusk he set out and met the German Commander and spent a long time pleading with him to spare the village. Then as they sat deeply involved in their discussion, suddenly they heard the voices of children singing. The children of Hunspach had followed their pastor, and they stood singing the folk songs of Alsace and also some of the psalms they had learned in the church. For over half an hour, the two men stood in silence, as the children sang and sang. Then at length the commander turned to the pastor and said, "I have learned tonight that I have a greater duty than my duty to my country, I have a duty to humanity. Your village will be spared." So the landmines were removed and the village and the people left in peace.

Sometimes whenever we read the Sermon on the Mount we are apt to think that it is a little over the top, indeed idealistic and impractical. Of course the real trouble is that we have so seldom tried to follow the teaching of Jesus. Consider some of the things he said:

"You have heard it was said, an eye for an eye and a tooth for a tooth. But I say unto you, do not resist evil. But if anyone strikes you on the right cheek, turn to him the other also; and if anyone sue you and take your coat, let him have your cloak as well; and if anyone forces you to go one mile, go with him two miles".

We here in Northern Ireland have to relearn what this teaching is about. Jesus in his teaching and indeed his life is not just outlining for us a few rules, but rather a total attitude to life. It is not just a code of practice but a positive dynamic outlook to permeate every part of life. It comprehends how we use all our talents and resources. There are no "duty free zones." It is not just about the current "troubles" but about our individual personal lives as well as our social and communal responsibilities.

Perhaps I can describe it as the Culture of Peace as against the Culture of Violence. Such a culture is not about the occasional visits to the local art gallery or concert of classical music. It covers every part of life: politics, religion, industry and education. It is about life-style, responsibility, and values. The Culture of Peace must embrace all we are and all we do.

We are only too well versed in the Culture of Violence. Indeed most of you who read this have never known a time without violence. We must be willing to identify and name what makes the Culture of Violence. Consider the lethal virus of prejudice and distrust that infects us all or the deadly bacteria of sectarianism that is so rampant in our culture.

One of the problems is with the word peace itself. It is a rather insipid and negative word merely indicating the absence of war and violence. But the dominant word for peace used in the Bible is the word shalom. It is a comprehensive word, covering the many relationships of daily life and expressing the ideal state of living in the community. Its basic meaning is totality, wholeness, well-being and harmony. It is a society in which the dignity and worth of each person is recognised and respected and where there are no second-class citizens. The various writers of both OT and NT emphasise that time after time God is a God of peace. He is the source of peace and that the coming of Christ was as the Prince of Peace.

Martin Luther King catches the authentic, positive, dynamic and Christ-like image of the true peacemaker in a speech he made shortly before he was assassinated:

"We will match your capacity to inflict suffering with our capacity to endure suffering. We will meet your physical force by soul force. We will not hate you, but cannot in all good conscience obey your unjust laws. We will soon wear you down by our capacity to suffer. And in winning our freedom, we will so appeal to your heart and conscience that we will win you in the process".

Love Grandad

HAS THE CHURCH HAD IT?

Dear Andrew, I know you are a historian and are familiar with the history of the early Church.

There is no doubt that now the Church does not get a very favourable press among young people. Many of them feel that it is irrelevant and out of date. But let's look at the facts. After all the Church has been in existence for some 2000 years and cannot be accused of being an upstart. Indeed it has outlived and outlasted many cultures and civilisations that have tried to destroy it. It had to face much persecution and many martyrdoms from the start. Actually it faced persecution for 129 years out of 249 at the beginning. Several Roman Emperors did their best to stamp out the Christian faith.

No doubt you have heard of Nero who "fiddled while Rome burned." He was responsible for the fire that destroyed a good part of Rome, but in order to allay the scandal, he blamed the Christians and punished them with the utmost cruelty. Besides being put to death they were made to serve as objects of amusement; they were clad in the hides of beasts and torn to death by dogs, others were crucified, others set on fire to serve to illuminate the night when daylight failed. This was only the beginning of what continued to happen over the first 300 years AD.

In spite of all these set-backs, the Church survived and grew. It was "a hammer that wore out many anvils." In fact the blood of the martyrs became the seed of the Church. But there were the dark periods as well as the light. G.K. Chesterton reminds us that there were at least four times in history when all the wisest minds in the world declared the Church to be dead.

First. When the first flush of the dawning faith had faded, the sagest minds in Rome said that the faith could not survive another 50 years.

Second. So it was when the Mohammedan Crescent was highest in the sky. The Holy Land fell, then Africa, then Asia Minor until the Moors were hammering on the central doors of Spain. Once more the Church seemed dead.

Third. So it was just before the Reformation when a parish priest could openly boast that he had never read the Gospel. When a child of two was appointed bishop, so that the relatives might draw the revenue from the diocese.

Fourth. So it was just before Wesley's time. When a man asked what day it was he got the reply that it must be Sunday, as there was a drunken fair in the town. And an English bishop refused the Chair of Canterbury because the fight against the rationalists seemed no longer worth it.

In 1816, Poet John Keats said of the churches, "They are dying like an outburnt lamp. But he forgot that the first essential of a quiet funeral is a willing corpse.

Sometimes you may feel that the church you have been associated with does not do much to excite or inspire you. But you have got to be careful in your judgement. For example, you may play football or hockey or rugby in a very poor club where the standard of play is terribly low. But you will not write off the thrill and fulfilment of those games, because your team is a bad one. You know that these are all great games and you'll want yourself and your team mates to do the game justice and play it as it should be played. This of course means being fit, training and discipline. In other words you'll not write off the Church Universal because yours is not a very inspiring example. You'll perhaps challenge the church you know to be the Church and decide to play your part and not just sit on the sidelines and criticise.

This is the tribute that Albert Einstein, the world famous Jewish scientist, paid to the Church in Germany in the Nazi times:

"When the revolution came to Germany, I looked to the universities to defend freedom, knowing that they boasted of their devotion to the cause of truth; but no, the universities were immediately silenced. Then I looked to the great editors of the newspapers and to the individual writers in Germany who had written much and often concerning the place of freedom in modern life; but they were mute. Only the churches stood squarely across the path of Hitler's campaign for suppressing truth. I have never had any special interest in the Church before but now I feel a great affection and admiration because the Church alone has had the courage and persistence to stand for intellectual truth and moral freedom."

Love Grandad

LIFE THROUGH DEATH

Dear Andrew, I want to share with you one of the most shattering and unforgettable experiences of my whole life

Early in 1944 I was travelling as a prisoner of war by train through the city of Dresden in Germany. I was escorted by a German soldier. On our journey out of the city we stopped at Neustadt in the suburbs. As I looked out of the window a great slogan written on the platform hoarding caught my eye and startled me to full attention, as it read "Wir werden England Coventrieren". I knew enough German to understand what it meant, that all England would be bombed as Coventry had been. This implied that the attack on Coventry in November 1940 had been from their point of view the most successful of all their attacks. Indeed this is verified in what Churchill wrote in his memoirs:

"The raid started early in the dark hours of the 14th, and by dawn nearly 500 German aircraft had dropped nearly 600 tons of high explosive and thousands of incendiaries. On the whole this was one of the most devastating raids that we sustained. The centre of Coventry was shattered and its life for a spell completely disrupted. Four hundred people were killed and many more seriously injured. The German radio proclaimed that our other cities would be similarly 'Coventrated'

The subsequent history is a remarkable story of reconstruction out of total destruction and it was typified by the building of a wonderful modern cathedral right inside the ruins of the old 12th Century one. It is an inspiring attempt not only to preserve the faith it has passed on to us through t   he centuries, but also to present it in a way that is meaningful to us in the 20th and 21st Century. Or as the architect, Sir Basil Spence, said: "to declare the presence of God with the finest means the 20th Century affords". From its opening its aim has been to promote a comprehensive programme that would face the challenges and demands of our time.

A splendid illustration of this - and it is where we in Corrymeela come into the story - is the world wide Cross of Nails programme, which has focussed not on Coventry but on places all over the world where there has been or is conflict. This programme has inspired and financed centres dedicated to the ministry of peace and reconciliation all over the world. Our Coventry House in Ballycastle reminds us each day not only of the marvellous generosity of Coventry, but also how real and practical their vision has proved to be. Since it was opened in 1976 it has been the home of hundreds of youth volunteers who come year by

year from all over the world to help to run the many programmes at the Centre on the theme of peace building and reconciliation.

But for me and I should think for most people, the most compelling feature is the remarkable tapestry behind the altar. It is of the Risen Christ. It is immense - some 75 by 39 feet. It is right in the centre and can be seen very clearly from any part of the cathedral. We can see that it dominates yet it unites all the other signs and symbols. Above all it gives the sense of a Presence who is at once radiant and powerful, compassionate yet awesome, gentle yet inescapable. Indeed King of Kings and Lord of Lords.

Yet this Christ is no ethereal or other worldly figure but rooted in the realities of our contemporary society, outlined in the ongoing life and programme of the cathedral. So often people think of the Christian Faith as geared to an age that is past, yesterday's world indeed. To me there is something very exciting and inspiring in the story of Coventry Cathedral. Is it not a living parable of hope and possibility? Think of the ancient Cathedral 900 years old, imagined and built by Christian people of that time. What an undertaking it was in terms of skill, time and labour. Remember what it must have meant to multitudes of people throughout the centuries.

Then in 1940 the hate and horror of WW2 saw its almost total destruction in a few hours. But that was not the end. True there was death and destruction but from that death there was resurrection and new life. Evil and hate do their best, but faith in the living Christ lives on, and new life, fresh vision and creative hope are reborn. There is indeed life through death!

Love Grandad

OVER TO YOU MATE, YOU HANDLE THIS

Dear Andrew, I'm sure you'll agree with me about the boredom of long prayers in church. You'll be glad to know you are not the only one.

After a lot of experience I vote for short prayers and on occasions very short! We have all suffered from long prayers and perhaps been 'turned off' by them'.Many years ago at a theological college one of the professors tended to indulge himself in long prayers. He would pray on and on and just when you thought he had reached a climax and end,he would start up again. One of the students very aptly described these prayers as 'a series of narrow escapes' and another comment was that the professor 'thought more on Eternity than Time'. I should comment that these prayers took place just before the evening meal and all the participants were very young and very hungry.

It is sad to consider the number of young people who have been put off belief, because at a crucial time in their lives they have had to listen to long and discursive prayers. Our Lord,himself,was very aware of this and put it very directly and forcefully when he was talking about the importance of prayer and how we ought to pray.

'And in praying do not heap up phrases as the Gentiles do, for they think that they will be heard for their many words'.

I am sure that very often the most important prayers are the very short ones, perhaps just a short sentence or one or two words. Such have been described as 'arrow prayers' swift and to the point. They are vital and real just because they spring spontaneously out of our immediate experience, whether it be of fear,wonder or joy. These are re-active and remind us how natural and human prayer is. Of course these instant prayers are only part of what prayer is about,but a very special part when we are apprentices and learners. The title of this letter is a good example of what I mean. I first came upon it when I was in a pretty miserable prison camp in Italy. One day I was talking to a fellow prisoner who was very seriously ill and he told me of this very simple prayer and what it meant to him at this time when he was so ill and very far from home. It was just these few words: 'Over to You Mate...You handle this.' To him and to all the others he lived with in the Camp,the word 'mate' had nothing slick or cheap about it. Your Mate was a very special person, one with whom you shared food and Red Cross parcels when they came. You spent much of your time together and walked round the perimeter track for exercise. He was one with whom you could share not only your food but your thoughts, longings and expectations for the future when you got home. Indeed a very special relationship! There have been many times during those days and since then when this arrow prayer has meant very much to me and I pass it on to you, because experience has taught me that it is for real.

I am convinced that many young people have the wrong idea about prayer. Sometimes they think of it as something formal and for set occasions. Indeed something that the priest or minister does. Of course that is part of it but it is something far bigger and comprehensive - something for all occasions!

I believe the essence of prayer is relationship. In fact what God wants us to have with Him. In this the most vital component is communication. The most tragic event in a marriage or a friendship or in a family is when those involved stop talking to one another because they have nothing to say and no common ground.

In contrast to this, consider how alive a real relationship can be. Those involved are always glad to be together and, as we say, 'be comfortable with each other'. From your own experience you'll know what this is like. There is the freedom to talk about everything. Sometimes you will argue and have different opinions; sometimes you will talk a lot and at other times you will say very little and just be content to be together in mutual respect and trust.

I am sure that some such feeling should be ours in praying. It too is about a continuous relationship which from day to day will embrace the whole of our lives. To me prayer is the blood-stream of faith. Think of any of the famous Christians of this century and you will see that it was the life-line or sheet-anchor of their existence in the hardest and most testing times.

Then again it often is the expression of the most profound longings and raw feelings. Read some of the psalms which often plumb the depths of human hopes and aspirations. The trials and problems as well as the joys of human experience were too real and profound to express in polite and carefully considered language.and modulated tones. Think for instance of the deep yearning for God there is in each one of us and the unforgettable way in which it is expressed in Psalm 42.

> 'As the deer longs for the running water,
> So longs my soul for you, O God
> My soul is thirsty for God, thirsty for the living God'.

There is one other thing that must be said here. Perhaps I have been misguided in speaking earlier of God as 'my Mate'. Some may think of this as cheap and out of place although I have tried to explain how real it was in the situation at that time. But it does help us to understand one of the most important truths of our faith. On the one hand His nearness and intimacy and at the same time His majesty and infinite greatness.

> 'This is how Oliver Wendall Holmes puts it in his hymn:

Lord of all being, throned afar,
Thy glory flames from sun and star;
Centre and soul of every sphere,
Yet to each loving heart how near'
    I love the way in which Mark Connolly describes it in his play 'Green Pastures'. He tells how God is at one moment creating a new constellation and in the next he is mending a sparrow's wing!

Love Grandad

PERCEPTION

Dear Andrew, Most of us are inclined to stereotype people and this story is a typical example.

I will never forget the first German soldier I saw close up. It was in the North African port of Tobruk just after it had been captured by the African Korps in June 1942. It was at a water point where he was filling some cans from the pump. I still clearly recall how fascinated I was, as he was so different from what I had expected. Indeed I could hardly take my eyes off him. He was so relaxed, as he chatted to those in charge.

As I thought about it I came to see what a set idea I had of the German soldier. I had read so much about them in the press and heard so much on the radio. I had in fact a stereotyped image in my mind of what such a person should look like - tough, ruthless, with his Nazi salute, leather jack boots, heel clicking and automatic "Heil Hitler" greeting. I had put all soldiers of the enemy in a set mould. I took some time to get over this, as I discovered he was very much like any of us.

That simple experience made me understand the importance of the way in which we perceive other people, the way we understand and think of them. This is a unique human quality - our capacity to respond and relate, to feel and think about others. It is the foundation of all of our relationships and it can be positive or negative, either binding people and communities or tearing them apart. The greatest danger to true perception is to stereotype, to classify people and communities.

This is to put them on what we would call stereo files according to class, background, education, religion, politics. Another word for this sort of thinking is prejudice; judging others by labels and not as real people. And in our divided society how many of us are free of pre-judging people in this way?

It is here that the approach of Christ is so relevant for us in Ireland. He was no other-worldly idealist, "He knew what was in man". He was the only truly perceptive man who ever lived, because, on the one hand he saw and in fact experienced the terrible depravity and evil of human nature, but, on the other hand, he saw the potential in every person to whom he related. Remember a few of those he met: the prostitute, the greedy tax collector, the criminal who hung beside him on the cross, the disciple who betrayed and denied him. He recognised who they were and the awful things that they had done. But he also saw the possibility in their lives as to what they could do and be.He perceived them and he perceives us not just as we are but what we may become!

Love Grandad

PERSPECTIVE

Dear Andrew, I know you are just back from a year in Japan, so I thought you would appreciate this piece.

When John Cole, the Political Editor of BBC, received an Honourary Doctorate from Queen's University, he told this story in his speech of acceptance. It was about the Old Derry and Lough Swilly Railway.

"In the old days railways were notorious among travellers in the North-West, through which it meandered, for a devil-may-care attitude to timetables, which made even the wilder sections of British Rail look positively Swiss in their punctuality. On one occasion, a traveller from the depths of Donegal, burdened by a large trunk and four suitcases, was being helped to the main station in Derry to catch his train to Belfast. The porter courteously inquired whether, with so much luggage, he was travelling far.

'Yes' said the traveller rather proudly, 'I am going to work in China'

The porter eyed him encouragingly and said, 'Ach well, Sir, at least ye've got the worst of your journey over ye'.

As I was thinking about this delightful story, I thought of photography and how in my enthusiasm I had invested in several types of lenses. There was the standard lens for close up pictures, the telephoto for distant shots and zoom for fast moving subjects and also the wide angle and the panoramic. Whatever else I learnt from these adventures in photography, I did in a new way understand the great number of different ways in which we can see the world around us and also the importance of our attitude to it.

For example, like our Donegal friend, we may be tempted to think only of our own little world, our own 'neck of the woods', and forget or ignore the wider world of which we are a part, rather like A.A. Milne's Christopher Robin.

'There's nobody else in the world today
  And the world was made for me'.

It's so easy to come to see the world just in terms of ourselves, our own people, our own class or denomination. So much modern culture fosters that attitude. This presents us with a great challenge of our time: to widen our horizons, to move from tunnel vision and short sightedness and be open to the great challenges of the world we inhabit and develop a panoramic or global way of seeing things. This is what the recent confrontation in Seattle was all about, as the world's 'have nots' are beginning to challenge the 'haves'.

But the real question we have to ask is about God's perspective. How does He see the world we inhabit? Does He only care about the good people - a select few?

Does He only care about 'our people' and 'our tradition' and not consider 'their people' and 'their tradition'? Is He concerned about colour or class?

Isn't this the most important and crucial question we humans can ask? How does He look at the world? How does He see things? The Bible, especially in the New Testament from beginning to end shouts out that He loves the world. This is the amazing and incredible master theme that runs right through the whole book. They are perfectly focussed for us in Paul's words to the Christians in Ephesus: 'He has made known to us the mystery of his will... which he purposed in Christ... to bring all things in Heaven and Earth together under one head, even Christ'

So often at Corrymeela we spell out the same truth as we sing the Negro spiritual:

'He's got the whole world in His hands'.

Love Grandad

ALIVENESS

Dear Caitlin, Have you ever seen a statue come alive?

Some time ago Granny and I were on holiday in Dublin and went to see a play in the Gate Theatre. 'Prunella' was the title of the drama, which was described as a romantic pantomime by Houseman and Barker. Truth to tell I cannot remember the details of the play. One thing, however, does stay in my mind after the years. From the raising of the curtain and right through the play there was a statue of a man in a very conspicuous position on the stage. Indeed as time passed, it seemed to dominate everything. Then suddenly in the final scene the statue started to move, at first very slowly, as the eyes began to blink and head to turn and the arms and legs seemed to loosen. 'It' was alive! There were gasps from the audience and I could feel an eerie feeling up my spine. Then we could see that the statue was a real live person. It was the same intense feeling that comes over you when you lift what you presume is a ball of wool and discover that it is a live mouse.

Frequently the Bible talks about people being alive or being dead and it is not in a physical but in a mental and spiritual sense. Being dead is to be apathetic, unwilling to respond. Think of the multitude of phrases currently used: to be 'browned off', 'bored to death', 'couldn't care less', 'so what', 'I don't want to know' – these all come from those who don't want to respond to life or be aware of what's going on in the real world. So they use all sorts of ways of escaping real life and living in their own cocoon, safely insulated from what is happening around them. Even a certain type of religion can do this and that is why John V. Taylor comments:

'It is my conviction that God is not hugely concerned about whether we are religious or not. What matters is whether we are alive or not'.

To be dead in this way is to be afraid of the hardships and challenges of life. When fear takes over we try to play safe and refuse to get involved, shutting our eyes both to the glory of life as well as its ugliness. We choose to be less alive in order to be less bothered, because awareness makes demands. It hurts, so we grow a protective shell and become a little blind, a little deaf, a little dead. Remember the Priest and the Levite in Jesus' parable about the traveller who fell among thieves. They passed by without noticing the victim at the side of the road. It is so easy to train oneself not to notice.

Jesus spoke very often about living and life. He said that he came to give life in all its fullness. John's gospel focusses on this time after time. "In him was life" and "I am the Way, the Truth and the Life." Somehow Jesus did not only teach about life: he transmitted it. How powerfully this comes through in the verdict of the disciples: "To whom shall we go, your words are words of eternal life."

What does this mean? When Jesus came, things began to happen. He didn't just talk and preach: he healed the sick, he fed the hungry, he gave sight to the blind, he raised the dead, he forgave sinners and he claimed to be the Messiah, the Son of God. His enemies conspired against him and he was crucified. But he was Life and on the cross Life conquered Death. So he is risen and alive for always. Death could not hold him.

One of the most remarkable people who ever came to Corrymeela was Bernard Brett. He was born with cerebral palsy (a spastic) in Belfast. He was never able to speak, walk or use more than one hand. He never attended school and was educated at home by his parents and partly through his own determination and quick mind. At 20 years he decided to go and live in a residential centre for adult spastics in Colchester. After seven years there, he moved into his own house where he lived until his death some twenty years later.

During this time his record was amazing. He gained an MA at Essex University for Social Policy and Administration. Then he founded a Christian Action Housing Association in North Essex for homeless families and unsupported mothers and others with social difficulties. He was secretary of this for many years. He also ran a Housing Advisory Service and as a result hundreds of people came to seek his help. In addition he ran an Adventure Playground Association and served on various national and local pressure groups for the handicapped and disadvantaged. Small wonder that he was awarded the MBE for his services.

Hard and painful experiences have come his way and this is what he wrote: "At some times I have felt the guiding hand of God, steering my life in certain directions and this is a very wonderful and rich experience. Yet at other times and for quite long periods I have known depression. Life seems an endless struggle and the prospect of having to live in the extreme limitations of my disabilities, with the knowledge that with the passing years they will become worse rather than better is a daunting thought. There are some mornings when I wake up during the depression, that I simply want to cease living. I have found this first-hand experience of depression unto the edge of suicide very helpful in trying to assist very depressed or suicidal people, because I have first-hand knowledge of what they are going through. The development of a relationship based on shared experience, can be the basis for beginning to give the despairing person hope, which is in my belief, much more important at times than giving people help.

As the years pass with growing speed, I feel increasingly strongly that we are all on a great journey of faith and time. How we use this life, which is the only one we can be certain about, is largely up to each one of us. I know very well that I have made many mistakes and actively damaged some people's lives in rather terrifying ways. The fact that I may have helped and guided quite a few other people's lives in their times of need, may not be so important. The hurt and evil we do can only be redeemed by the Love and Grace of Christ.

Yet for all the mistakes I may have made and will continue to make, I know that each one of us has the opportunity and the divine gift of being able to grow into more full and loving human beings, if we allow the Spirit of God to work in the yeast of our inner being."

Love Grandad

THE GREATEST DRAMA EVER STAGED

Dear Caitlin, You have always been keen on acting so I thought this story of "The Greatest Drama Ever Staged" would appeal to you.

This is the title of a small booklet by Dorothy Sayers, a household name some years ago for her detective novels featuring the activities of the super sleuth, Lord Peter Wimsey. That, however, was only one part of her claim to fame, because she also distinguished herself as a playwright, broadcaster, theologian and scholar. It is fascinating to note that she worked for a time with an advertising firm and was responsible for two very famous Guinness advertisements. One was of a very contented Penguin with a glass of Guinness half way down its throat and the distraught zoo keeper looking on in despair and uttering: "My Goodness, My Guinness".

The other was of a very prosperous Toucan with his enormous beak straddling two pints of Guinness and underneath the caption:

"If he can say as you can

Guinness is good for you.

How grand to be a Toucan

Just think of what Toucando."

By way of contrast one of her most remarkable achievements was to write a series of radio plays on the life of Christ - "The Man born to be King". This was just before television came. The plays had a remarkable impact and were repeated again and again. The Director of Religious Broadcasting commented: "These plays have done more for preaching the Gospel to the unconverted than any effort of the churches or religious broadcasting since the last war"

The most memorable of her writings was a small booklet - "The Greatest Drama ever Staged". In this she slams the ever current impressions that religion is dull, boring and irrelevant. "If this is dull, then what in Heaven's name can be called exciting? The people who hanged Christ, never, to do them justice, accused him of being a bore - on the contrary they thought him too dynamic to be safe".

But isn't there far more to it than that? There is the crucial choice we have all got to make for ourselves, whether it was true or false. Because if it really is true and these things really happened, then it is indeed the greatest drama ever staged and the most important thing that has ever happened!

Think of what it means - that God really cares for us and for this world he has made. Again and again the Bible tells us that God is love and that He loves you and me and the whole of His creation. We cannot understand why He loves us. Perhaps we can think of Him as a truly creative artist who made us as the expression of His love and His nature so that we can share it with Him and with one another. He made us like himself with the ability to think, to understand and also free to choose how we will live. He does not force or compel. He lets us choose. So we can decide whether we live in community with God and our fellows or choose 'to do our own thing'. That is what the first story in the Bible is about - the story of the first man and woman, and it is your story and mine. By and large people have chosen like the Prodigal to live for themselves because they think they know best.

But that is only the first act of the drama. It now becomes the greatest rescue story ever staged. God decides to make the next move - to go into the world Himself. So He comes to live amongst us in Jesus Christ. In Him we see the meaning and purpose of life and how we ought to live our lives. Think of the way He put it "I am come to give you life and more life than before". But it didn't work out. After some interest at the start, He was deserted and indeed betrayed to his enemies and it all seemed to be the end of another well-meaning idealist.

But then there is a great twist in the plot. He is crucified - an indescribable slow, agonising and utterly humiliating death by inches. But the incredible thing was that he died undefeated, forgiving his murderers, consoling his friends and bringing new life to the thief on the Cross beside him and finally praying for his killers - "Father forgive them for they know not what they do".

But that was not the end but really the beginning of the drama. The final act of the play transforms the whole story. After three days he rises from the grave and comes back as the conqueror of death, the destroyer of evil, hate, selfishness and pride. He comes as the one who brings meaning, hope and fulfilment to those who follow him. Multitudes of every age and generation proclaim that today.

But this is the question I ask myself and I ask you, as we listen to this story of the Man of Nazareth. Do I really believe it - do you really believe it? Because it is indeed THE GREATEST DRAMA EVER STAGED.

Love Grandad

ON BEING TOTALLY PRESENT

Dear Caitlin, I wonder what your pet aversion is?

Everyone of us has his own special aversions and dislikes. One of mine is whenever I have to attend a social function such as a wedding, a graduation or some other occasion and an acquaintance approaches you and begins to talk. Then just as you are getting into your stride he stops and begins to look away from you exclaiming, 'Oh, there is old so-and-so. I must have a word with him. He rushes off leaving your conversation in mid-air and you are left with the impression that the other person is not very interested in you or your conversation. In other words that person is not 'totally present with you'. His mind is on other things and other people and the result is that you feel rather diminished.

This unwillingness or inability to be totally present to the time and the situation in which we live can be expressed in different ways. For instance there are those who choose to live their lives in the past. Perhaps this is a special temptation for the older generation. They have developed the habit of looking back to the old days that they become imprisoned in them. Perhaps this is partly understandable in a time of so much change, so rapid and so bewildering. But this attitude is not confined to the older people. This is all too clear in our situation in Northern Ireland where such a large number of people refuse to recognise the need for change. They still have not learnt that history does not move backwards and that change is a vital part of living and we should not be afraid of it. We have indeed to learn to be alive to the time in which we live. This is not 1690 or 1916!

But the other side of that is to live completely in the future and to have a Utopian attitude. The person who perpetually lives in the 'if only' world. Those who all the time are building castles in the air which they know and we know will never be occupied.The danger is that such thinking can become a means of avoiding real responsibility and of doing anything practical about the problem. This is the danger of the sentimentalist when feelings become a substitute for deeds.

Don't get me wrong here. Of course the past and the future are important. But it is all important to keep the balance. One of the few things I remember my father saying to me, especially when I was worried about approaching examinations, was the importance of doing a day's work each day and leaving the future to look after itself.

Consider these lines from the Sanscrit - the ancient language of India:

'Today is the very life of life.
In its brief course lie all activities
And realities of your existence
The bliss of youth,
The splendour of beauty,
The glory of action.
Yesterday is but a dream,
Tomorrow is only a vision,
But today well lived will make
Every yesterday a dream of happiness
And each tomorrow a vision of hope.
So look ye well therefore to this day
This is the salutation of the dawn.'

This is how it is expressed in the Taize rule:

'Be present to the time in which you live; adapt yourself to the conditions of the moment.

Love the dispossessed, all those who, living amid man's injustice, thirst for justice.'

Love Grandad

RING A RING O'ROSES

Dear Caitlin, You may remember singing this nursery rhyme in your kindergarten days.

Have you ever asked just what the words mean? Anyway behind it there is a sad yet wonderful story. It dates away back to 1665 when Charles II was King and it is about a little village called Eyam in Derbyshire.

The village tailor had received a box of cloth from London at his home. From this he hoped to make clothes for different people, but it was never to be, for within two days the tailor was very ill with a raging fever and strange swellings developing into a rosy rash all over his body. When he died a great fear came over the other villagers, as they realised that the terrible plague had arrived from London. This had already killed many in the overpopulated streets of the city. It was a bacterial disease that had been carried by rats coming in by ships from the east. Doctors did all they could with what medicine they had and also by quarantining sufferers and their relatives. Healthy and sick were shut up together, their doors being marked with a red cross.

Several strange cures were tried but none more strange than the suggestion that the people should carry nosegays or posies to ward off the plague. Hence the nursery rhyme:

Ring a ring o'roses
A pocket full of posies
Atishoo, atishoo
And we all fall down.

The Rector of Eyam, William Mompesson, rose to the occasion and gave his people a noble lead in the crisis. He was very afraid that the plague would spread out over all of Derbyshire and far beyond. He thought carefully about what could be done and then together with his non-conformist colleague, Thomas Stanley, called the villagers together and explained the situation. Then he did a truly heroic thing. He challenged the villagers to a great act of self sacrifice: to shut themselves up with the plague in order to stop it from spreading to the surrounding villages.

The people agreed to what for many of them would be a death sentence. A stone circle was put around the village to mark the boundary. It was agreed that food would be left here at various points. Money to pay for it was put in running water. The village was sealed off. Plague victims were buried in their own gardens or in the fields. Week by week the death list grew in the parish register, as household after household fell victim to the plague. It took 15 months for the plague to die in the hard winter of 1666. By then the total was 260 dead out of 350 inhabitants.

This Is an incredibly moving story of the wonderful courage of one man and the marvellous response of his congregation and how through their supreme self-sacrifice thousands of lives were saved from the ravages of the plague. But it is more - it is an action parable for us today here in Northern Ireland, living in a society that is infected by another virulent plague. It is not one that affects the body but the minds of multitudes in our small country. It keeps on breaking out in different places when families are driven from their homes, houses are set on fire, churches and chapels vandalised and worst of all in the terrible loss of life. All because of this deadly plague of hatred, fear and distrust.

We have much to learn from the people of Eyam. They were ordinary people who got together and saw how they could save the lives of multitudes of others. They counted the cost and literally gave themselves for others. Indeed they died that others might live. I find this story from an obscure English village deeply challenging.

Corrymeela and many other peace organisations are committed to the work of peace and the destruction of sectarianism, but if this is to be defeated, it will take the dedication and self sacrifice of everyone. That means the work, the courage, the sacrifice, and the commitment of each one of us. Real peace will come but it begins with you and with me.

Let each one of us work out the actions we can take - whether great or small - that will save our country from this deadly virus.

Love Grandad

THE ROAD TO DOMODOSSELA

Dear Caitlin, I'm sure you have no idea where Domodossela is, so let me tell you about it.

Some years ago several of us from Corrymeela were invited to spend a holiday in Switzerland. Our home was at Casa Locarno, a beautifully appointed ecumenical centre commanding a wonderful panorama of the town stretched out below and Lake Locarno, encircled with various mountain ranges. It was a breath-taking sight and a well run programme which gave us plenty of time to relax and get to know our fellow guests who came from both sides of the then Iron Curtain. Very quickly we settled in and got to know the others, many of whom had fascinating accounts of how they had been able to come to Switzerland.

One afternoon the three of us - Billy McAllister, Warden of Corrymeela, Granny and I decided that we would like to explore the district and set off on a trip by the narrow-gauge railway through what was called "The Hundred Valleys". We would have time to do the journey to a place called Pontebrolla and be back for the evening meal. This seemed an excellent idea and we set out in eager anticipation, and the most spectacular scenery did not disappoint us. After about an hour's journey the train began to slow down and stopped. Alas, it was only then that we realised that we had arrived at our destination. We hastened to collect our bags and rushed to the door at the end of the carriage. To our horror we were unable to get the door open. Apparently there was an electric button to open the door, but we did not know how to operate it. To our dismay the train started and we had to stay on.

It turned out to be a costly mistake, as the train did not stop until we had crossed the border into Italy about an hour and a half later. Finally we came to a stop at a town called Domodossala. After a two hour wait we caught the train back to Locarno, duly chastened, quite tired and hungry. We were grimly determined that in future we would make sure that we knew when and how to get off!

I have often thought of that experience and it seems to me to be a parable of how we ought and ought not to live our lives. It is all too easy to live like that, not really thinking of 'getting on' or 'getting off' and leaving it to others to decide for us. Indeed so much of our current culture is geared to that idea, that most people simply conform, go with the crowd, and are content for others to set their agenda and make their decisions.

Ours is a very intensive current culture and it is reinforced by the tremendous power of modern technology which has access to the heart

of every home. It is largely materialistic, offers almost instant satisfaction, and it encourages viewers to look after themselves and their interests. It is based on the lowest common denominator: money, rivalry and sex.

But then there is that other culture that points the other way. It proclaims that we are members of one another, that we are part of a larger whole and mutually dependent. Indeed we need each other to survive. John Donne living in the 17th Century reminds us how interdependent we are:

"No man is an island entire of itself; every man is a piece of the continent, a part of the main. Any man's death diminishes me, because I am involved in Mankind and therefore never send to know for whom the bell tolls; it tolls for thee"

How then do we live our lives? Are we to be content to drift along and leave it to others to decide how we live? Or are we prepared to make our own choices, to create our own culture? That means that we are ready to do our own thing and break out of the mould and think for ourselves. I like the J.B. Phillips translation of a sentence from Paul's letter to the Romans:

"Don't let the world around you squeeze you into its own mould"

Let me put it in a nut shell:

There are three classes of people - those who make things happen, those who watch things happen, those who wonder what happened!

Love Grandad

USE OF THE IMAGINATION

Dear Caitlin, This is a wonderful example of the power of the imagination.

Some years ago Victor Gollanz was a very well known publisher. But he was in himself quite a remarkable person with a very deep concern for his fellows. During the last war he used to go to different places speaking about the horrors of the concentration camps that existed in Germany and the inhuman treatment that the inmates had to endure especially those who like himself were Jewish. He described in one of his books how he prepared himself whenever he had to speak about these camps. He would arrive at least an hour before the meeting was due to begin, would slip into a dark room by himself and sit there very quietly for most of the hour, trying to imagine what it was like to be a prisoner in Buchenwald or Belsen. In his imagination he could see the inmates dressed in their striped rags, he could hear the moans and cries, he could smell the putrid atmosphere and he could feel the desolation and despair. Then he would leave the room and go in and speak at the meeting. Each time he was able to speak with tremendous power and conviction and somehow enabled his listeners to feel and experience what it felt like to live in such a place.

If we want our faith to be vital and alive, it is not enough just to use our minds. We must also use our imagination, especially in reading the Bible, in worship in church or chapel and very especially in our prayers. If you really want the Bible to come alive it is all important to be able to identify with the various characters and feel ourselves into the story as it happens.

For example, one of the most memorable worships I was ever at, took place at Corrymeela. It was a fine sunny day, so we decided to hold it out of doors in the playground. It was Palm Sunday and a group of families were in the House for the week-end. The leaders decided that it had to be special and so as well as reading the passage about Christ's entry into Jerusalem, they decided that with all the children they would re-live the story. It happened that at that time there was a real donkey at Corrymeela.

Of course it took a lot of preparation. Branches with leaves had to be collected in Glenshesk. Light yellow nylon sheets were ideal for the participants and special hymns were practiced. Naturally it had its awkward and funny moments, as when the donkey trod on the foot of one of the boys who was leading it. But even he did not make too much fuss of it.

I will never forget the sight of that amazing procession coming down the hill from Cedar Haven. I was deeply moved by the reverence and dignity with which each of the children acted. Above all I can still see the fair-haired boy, representing Christ, and the solemn and un-forgettable way in which he played his part, completely living out the story. Then when the procession had arrived among the trees round the playground, the story was read aloud. Somehow for all the players and those of us who stood by, it had become far more than a play, but a living experience for all of us - players and viewers alike.

Love Grandad

A TIME TO SPEAK

Dear Charlotte, I know you have met Helen Lewis and read her book "A Time to Speak" so I am sending this account I have written about it and why it is so important.

This is the title of one of the most disturbing, challenging and thought-provoking books I have ever read. It is the unvarnished truth about human nature and describes the unspeakable things that we human beings can do to each other. It reminds me of the verdict of that arch-realist, Winston Churchill, writing long before the war.

"Under sufficient stress, starvation, terror, warlike passion or even cold intellectual frenzy, the modern man we know so well will do the most terrible deeds and his modern woman will back him up".

Helen Lewis who now lives in Belfast is the author and has written this book a very long time after the events described in it. In a recent speech she explained why. "Outside my closest family I did not and could not talk about my experiences in the camps, but I learned gradually to cope with the past, even if I sometimes felt isolated by my memories. It was a slow process of recovery until it was time to speak". She writes with great restraint and objectivity and lets the truth, witnessed truth, make its own impact and it is this that makes it so sobering and challenging. How would you and how would I have handled such a terrible situation? Helen raises many unanswerable questions.

Why did she survive and multitudes of others, braver and stronger, perish? Her answer is given by her response - to tell the story about those who lived and those who died - to share her experience of what happened so that we can see and judge for ourselves.

Helen had a very happy youth in Trutnov at the foot of the giant mountains in North East Bohemia. She was an only child. Both her parents moved in a highly cultured society and were very much in touch with the musical world. Her father died when she was eighteen and in her last year at school. Afterwards she moved with her mother to Prague and started studying Philosophy at the German University. Her real interest was, however, in the Art of Dance and from her early childhood her ambition was to be a Dancer. Dance to her was a vocation. There was nothing superficial or cheap about it. To her it is one of the supreme expressions of the human spirit. It involves one's total being - body, mind and spirit.

In the late thirties, having finished her Dance education at a very good Dance College that was based on the teachings of Rudolf Laban, she was well launched on a distinguished career and had already made quite a reputation for herself. She was very happily married to Paul and life seemed to hold great promise for her. Then her whole world collapsed. In March 1939 Hitler and the Nazis annexed the country. Very rapidly the SS and Gestapo apparatus got into action. Overnight public parks, swimming pools, theatres, cinemas, restaurants were forbidden to Jews. All Jews had to wear a yellow star to mark them out and isolate them from the rest of society. Very soon the Nazi aim became brutally clear - simply to liquidate all opposition and especially the Jews. The procedure was cynically cruel and simple. Words that came to have an awesome significance began to circulate such as the word "transport". First there was talk of a special Jewish Ghetto occupying the town of Terezin. But this was only a stage on the journey that led to a place called Auschwitz.

In August 1942 Helen was deported with Paul to Terezin and from there in May 1944 to Auschwitz from henceforth becoming a number - BA677. Her mother was deported in May 1942 to Sobibor, from where no one ever came back. In August 1944 Paul was sent from Auschwitz to Schwarzheide in Germany and Helen to Stutthof near the Baltic Sea. Her book then details all she experienced through 1943 and '44; the hunger, overcrowding, the filth, mindless cruelty and the sense of utter hopelessness, the rapid decline of her health after a perforated appendix and being at the point of death several times.

At the beginning of 1945 (27th January) in the last few weeks of the war she was caught up in the terrible Death March from Stutthof, to avoid the advancing lines of the victorious Red Army. In the depths of winter ice and snow they were forced to march on and on. This is how she described it: "After a few days it became clear that we were walking in ever decreasing circles. If our German guards had been rational they would have run away and saved themselves from the approaching Red Army but they just kept on blindly obeying orders to the last, to hate, torment and in the end to kill us"

This forced march lasted for two weeks until finally they were pushed into a deserted barn in the middle of nowhere. Here they were tormented by dysentery and lice. Many at this point simply gave up the struggle and lay down in a long line near the door with their faces covered by their blanket and waited for death. One morning she felt so ill and far gone that she struggled to her feet, took up her blanket and lay down with the dying. Her friends did what they could to change her mind but when she made no response they sighed, gave up and left her to die.

Then one evening like a sleep walker she got up, lifted her blanket and climbed painfully back to her former place among those who were determined to live. "I had had no blinding revelation, no inner voice had talked to me, no gentle hand had guided me and yet I had gone back among the living." This was a crucial choice for her - to live and not to die.

Suddenly, in the middle of the same night the light was switched on and a hysterical voice screamed at them to get up, to dress and line up outside the door in no more than five minutes. "We are moving on", it added with an alarming touch of panic. In no time they had obeyed, stood in rows of five, were counted and marched off. All except those lying at the entrance, where Helen had been, who waited to die.

Some hours later her group was driven back to the barn. With unspeakable horror they found the whole row at the door had been bayoneted to death. Helen's group had been recalled to bury the bodies and to conceal any sign of the massacre so that the Red Army would not find them. The barn itself was then burnt down.

This is one part of Helen's story but she does not leave us there. In the midst of all the horror, brutality and utter darkness shafts of light keep breaking through often from the most unexpected places. I can only touch on several stories of incredible kindness and bravery.

There was the new SS guard who arrived to supervise their work-party. The prisoners watched him very fearfully to see what he'd do to them. In the middle of the morning Helen jumped with alarm, as he pointed his finger at her and shouted: "You there, watch out". Something came flying through the air and landed at her feet. "Pick it up and open it and eat it right away". Helen did this and was amazed to find two well filled thick sandwiches. Later on they all realised that something extraordinary was happening. Every night the same SS man kept part of his meal to give it next day to some starving prisoner. He always made sure that it went to a different person each day and he always dispatched it through the air, as if to say that it wasn't from him but from up there.

To me the most incredible story in the book is when she risked her life jumping into a snowdrift to escape from her column of prisoners and was fortunate enough not to have been seen and shot.

She was just about able to stumble to a nearby farm house and find refuge there. Then a high ranking Russian officer arrived, listened to her story, made sure she got all the medical help possible and then provided a marvellous meal for her and did everything within his power to assure her that she would be able to return home in safety. The following day before he left, he wrote a message on a slip of pink paper that was to be the vital talisman in enabling her to get a safe passage home. Finally he made one of his officers promise that he would do all in his power to help her reach a place of safety. Soon after, she managed to travel back home to Prague and begin to recover her health and strength.

This book simply asks questions that apply to us all about good and evil. There is no attempt to give answers. We are presented with the awesome reality of evil and the wonder of goodness and we are left to make our own response. It provides no easy answers like the end of a fairy tale: "And they all lived happily ever after". This was not the experience of Auschwitz.

What does it say to us here in Northern Ireland? Supremely it underlines the perils of apathy and indifference about the social and political problems we face. It warns us about what can happen when people refuse to take responsibility for their community and refuse to become involved in anything but their own private lives and interests. We cannot remain content to opt out, to be neutral and unconcerned.

If we are to have a just and peaceful community, each of us has to play our part in the political and social structures so that justice, freedom and peace will prevail.

Love Grandad

AN EASTER EGG

Dear Charlotte, I hope you have a chance to visit Israel, as your mother did when she was a student.

In August 1942 I had the experience of a life time. I was able to visit Israel or Palestine, as it was called at that time. I spent most of the ten days in and around Jerusalem. I have vivid memories of the many places I saw and of course one of the most memorable was to visit the Mount of Olives and Gethsemane. I can still remember those very ancient olive trees along the rough tracks and the atmosphere of peace and quiet all around. As I paused and looked down I could see across the Kidron Valley and then up to the walls of the city and the Temple. Slowly I walked on up the Mount of Olives and soon I found myself at a beautiful Russian Church that looked down on the garden of Gethsemane. The church was square in shape with lofty spires at each corner and with roofs painted in gold and all suggesting life and hope. Inside the church the first thing I noticed was the huge curtain that shut off the altar and was only opened on special occasions when a service was going on.

One thing immediately that attracted my attention was a large picture hanging above the curtained altar. A young Russian nun explained the painting to me. In the centre of the picture a young woman in Eastern dress was kneeling down before the throne of the Roman Emperor who was sitting in state with various attendants around him. But the young woman was the central feature. Her face was very beautiful and radiant with an inner joy and serenity.

As I got closer I could see that she was holding something in her hand and showing it to the Emperor. It was an egg painted bright red. As she holds it up she seems to be explaining something to the Emperor who is listening very intently. After I had looked at the picture for some time the Russian nun began to explain it to me. Behind the picture there is a story. Mary Magdalene is the young woman and after the death and resurrection of our Lord she determined that she would do all she could to make sure that the whole world should know about what had happened. So she decided to go to the heart of civilisation, to Rome and indeed to the Emperor himself and tell the story of Christ to him.

We can imagine her travels and how much she had to do to get to Rome and see the Emperor. At length her persistence was rewarded and she was granted an audience with the Emperor. Of course she had thought very often of what she would say and do when she got the chance to see him. As she thought about this she got the brilliant idea of explaining the story with a coloured egg. So when the time came she went in and bowed to the Emperor.

Then she told the story of Christ. She described his deeds of love and his message. She told of those who opposed him, conspired to destroy him and finally had him crucified. But then she went on to tell the story of the Resurrection and how he had overcome the power of evil and hate and was risen and alive. Then she used the egg to illustrate her story. How on the one hand it seems so inert and lifeless but yet inside it has the power and promise of new life. Remember this story when you celebrate Easter with an Easter Egg.

Love Grandad

CAMERA LESSONS

Dear Charlotte, Like your Dad you are interested in cameras and know how rapidly they are changing, as all sorts of new models are being made.

I got very interested some years ago and invested in several different types of lenses such as the wide-angle, the telephoto and the zoom But now the arrival of the video camera has changed everything. It is much more flexible to use and has made the whole art of photography more simple and available. And moving pictures are for most of us much more interesting than stills. There is a vast difference between the static and dynamic view of things.

But this distinction applies far beyond photography and is most useful in helping us to understand what our faith is really like. I am sure that a great amount of misunderstanding of religion is due to the way in which it is so often presented as something that is always static and not dynamic.

That was the impression I got when as a young boy I learnt the Catechism of my church. In this the answer given to the question - 'Who is God?' reads 'God is a spirit infinite, eternal and unchangeable in his being wisdom, power, holiness, justice, goodness and truth'. Surely a very static picture.

Think of the vivid, active and living picture of God in the Old Testament. The God who leads his people from slavery to freedom. This God is a pillar of cloud by day and of fire at night. His spirit moves on the face of the water. This is one who permeates the whole of life, challenging and disturbing. Yet at the same time giving support and comfort. God's revelation, in a word, is not what the cinema trade calls a series of 'stills'. It is a moving picture. It is a drama giving meaning by its movement. So in the Bible the movement of events is the instrument through which truth is conveyed.

This is a modern parable called Sheriff/Scout.

THE CHURCH. In settler theology the church is the courthouse. The old stone structure dominates the town square. Inside its walls records are kept, taxes are paid, and trials are held for bad guys. It is the symbol of security, law, and order.

In Pioneer theology the church is the covered wagon. It is a house on wheels - always on the move. It bears the marks of life. It creaks, is scarred with arrow marks, and bandaged with bailing wire. The covered wagon is always where the action is.

GOD. In settler theology God is like the mayor. He smokes big cigars and lounges comfortably in an overstaffed office.

No one dares to approach him. Guys in black hats fear him, guys in white hats rely on him to keep things under control.

In Pioneer theology God is like a trail boss. He is rough and rugged and full of life. He lives and fights with his men. Without him the pioneers would become fat and lazy. He often gets down in the mud with the pioneers to help push the wagon when it gets bogged down.

JESUS. In settler theology Jesus is the sheriff. He is the guy sent by the mayor to enforce the rules. He wears a white hat and always outdraws the bad guys. He also decides who is thrown into jail.

In pioneer theology Jesus is the scout. He rides out ahead to find out which way the pioneers should go. He lives all the dangers of the trail. He doesn't ask the pioneers to do anything he didn't do first. His spirit and guts serve as a model to all.

CHRISTIAN. In settler theology the Christian is the settler. His concern is to stay out of the sheriff's way. He tends a small garden. His motto is 'Safety First'. To him the courthouse is a symbol of security, order and happiness.

In pioneer theology the Christian is the pioneer. He is the man of risk and daring, hungry for adventure, new life. He is tough, rides hard, and knows how to handle himself through trials and dangers. He enjoys the challenge of the trail. He dies with his boots on.

FAITH. In settler theology faith is trusting in the safety of the town, obeying the laws, believing the mayor is always in the courthouse and keeping your nose clean.

In pioneer theology faith is the spirit of adventure. It is the readiness to move out, to risk everything on the trail.

SIN. In settler theology sin is breaking one of the town's ordinances.

In pioneer theology sin is wanting to turn back.

Love Grandad

DOES GOD CARE?

Dear Charlotte, Helen Waddell was one of the most illustrious pupils in Victoria College, the school your Granny attended.

She was a very well known Ulster scholar and writer. She studied at Victoria College in the twenties and later at Oxford, where she specialised in medieval history and wrote several books. The best known were 'The Wandering Scholars' and 'The Story of Peter Abelard'. The last was a story of a very controversial philosopher and theologian who lived in the 12th Century. His whole life was moulded by his love for Heloise and how, because of his relationship with her, he had to leave the priesthood.

He was a very creative and profound thinker and this following extract takes us to the heart of his understanding of what God is like. He and his companion, Thibault, are passing along the Arduzon Valley in France. After a long walk they have decided to stop and prepare their evening meal.

Thibault was too happy for speech. He was busy unroping the little barrel and Abelard had risen, the segment of cheese in his hand, to reach down their drinking-horns from the wall, when both men suddenly stood still.

"My God," said Thibault "What's that?"

From somewhere near them in the woods a cry had arisen, a thin cry, of such intolerable anguish that Abelard turned dizzy on his feet, and caught at the wall.

"It's a child's voice," he said. "Oh, God, are they at a child?" The scream came back yet again.

"A rabbit" said Thibault. He listened "There's nothing worrying it. It will be in a trap. Hugh told me he was putting them down. "Christ" The scream came back yet again.

Abelard was beside him and the two plunged down the bank.

"Down by the river," said Thibault. "I saw them playing, God help them, when I was coming home. You know the way they become demented with fun in the evenings. It will have been the drumming with his hind paws to itself, that brought down the trap.

Abelard went on hardly listening "Oh God" he was muttering "Let it die quickly." but the cry came yet again. On the right, this time. He plunged through the thicket of hornbeam.

"Watch out." said Thibault, thrusting past him. "The trap will take the hand off you"

The rabbit stopped shrieking when they stooped over it, either from exhaustion or in some last extremities of fear. Thibault held the teeth of the trap apart, and Abelard gathered the little creature in his hands. It lay for a moment breathing quickly, then in some blind recognition of kindness at the last, the small head thrust and nestled against his arm, and it died.

It was the last confiding trust that broke Abelard's heart. He looked down at the little draggled body, his mouth shaking "Thibault" he said, "Do you think there is a God at all? Whatever has come to me I have deserved, but what did this one do?"

Thibault nodded.

"I know," he said. "Only, I think God is in it too"

Abelard looked up sharply.

"In it?" Do you mean that it makes Him suffer the way it does us?"

Again Thibault nodded.

"Then why doesn't he stop it?"

"I don't know" said Thibault. "Unless - unless it's like the Prodigal Son. I suppose the father could have kept him at home against his will. But what use would that have been? All this, he stroked the limp body, is because of us but all the time God suffers. More than we do."

"Thibault, do you mean Calvary?"

Thibault shook his head. "That was only a piece of it - the piece that we saw - in time. Like that. He pointed to a fallen tree beside them, sawn through the middle. "That dark ring there, it goes up and down the whole length of the tree, but you only see it when it is cut across". That is what Christ's life was; the bit of God that we saw. And we think God is like that for ever, because it happened once, with Christ. But not the pain. Not the agony at the last. We think that stopped."

Abelard looked at him, the blunt nose and the wide mouth. He could have knelt before him.

"Then, Thibault", he said slowly, "you think that all this", he looked down at the little quiet body in his arms, "all the pain of the world, was Christ's cross?"

"God's cross", said Thibault. "And it goes on"

"But, O God, if it were true. Thibault, it must be. At least there is something at the back of it that is true. Thibault, it must be. And if we could find it - it would bring back the whole world."

"I couldn't ever rightly explain it" said Thibault. But you could, if you would think it out." He reached out his hand, and stroked the long ears. "Old lopears," he said. "Maybe this is why he died. Come and have your supper, Master Peter... we will bury him somewhere near the oratory. In Holy ground."

Love Grandad

THE LOVE THAT CHANGED THE WORLD

Dear Charlotte, I'm sure you, like all of us, love a good romantic love story.

Every media producer knows that there is nothing more popular than a good love story. Indeed most of our greatest literature and drama draw their inspiration from this timeless theme. Consider the immortal stories of Dante and Beatrice or Heloise and Abelard or, of course, Romeo and Juliet!

But there is for me a love story that tops them all. Its setting was in the ancient kingdom of Israel away back in 750 BC. It is the story of one of Israel's greatest prophets, Hosea, who lived in Galilee. It is believed that he was a baker by trade. The big event in his early life was his love for Gomer. Alas, his happiness was as 'a morning cloud, as the dew that passes away early'. Very soon he discovered that Gomer did not return his love and had gone off with other lovers. Indeed she had sold herself as a temple prostitute. It would have been the custom in those days that he would throw her out and forget about her. Indeed that was what was expected in such a situation.

But he discovered that in spite of all that she had done and all the pain and suffering she had brought on him, he just could not give her up and forget about her. Eventually he learns that she has been deserted and her lovers have left her. He goes out and looks for her, finds her and buys her back from her masters. Still she did not respond to his love and as far as the story goes, she never did; but still his love goes on!

Then suddenly Hosea's tragic personal experience took on an amazing new meaning for him. He began to see that this was how his people and nation has treated God. In spite of all the marvellous things He had done for them in delivering them from slavery in Egypt, bringing them through all the hazards of the desert and bringing them as a people into the Promised Land of Israel. In spite of all, they had turned their backs on Him and followed false gods.

Yet in spite of all that had happened God would not give them up and still goes on loving, caring and longing for them to come back to him. These lines from Hosea seem to bring us to the high water mark of the Old Testament in grasping what God is really like. Are there any more moving and plaintive words in the Bible than Hosea's description of God's love for Israel.

"When Israel was a child I loved him as a son and brought him out of Egypt. But the more I called to him, the more he rebelled, sacrificing to Baal and offering incense to idols. I trained him from infancy, I taught him to walk. I held him in my arms. But he does not know nor even care that it was I who raised him. As a man who leads his favourite ox so I led Israel with my rope of love.

Oh, how can I give you up, my Ephriam? How can I let you go? How can I forsake you like Admah and Zeboiim? My heart cries out within me, how I long to help you"

To me this is one of the great high marks of the Old Testament and surely Hosea of Galilee is very close to Jesus of Nazareth!

Love Grandad

THE POWER OF WORDS

Dear Charlotte, I know young people prefer e-mails today but this is how an ordinary letter saved a man's life.

Peter Hartley was a prisoner in one of those awful Japanese camps. In his book he tells of the incredible ordeal of suffering he and his fellow prisoners had to pass through, building a railway through the jungle. Then one day he found that he simply could not go on, his body was powerless with fever and a few days later he suffered a crippling attack of dysentery. The doctors did all they could, but as the days passed he grew weaker and weaker. By the tenth day his spirit began to sink. He had no fight left and he was sure that he was dying. Then he began to pray that the end would come quickly.

Next morning he described how the orderly brought in the mail. He watched the letters being distributed without interest or curiosity. What use were letters now to a man about to die? What use were they, months or even years out of date.

Then suddenly the orderly threw a small packet of letters on his bed and said: "Somebody must love you, sergeant, to send all that lot." Hartley made no reply. He was debating whether he would look at them. This went on for several minutes and then suddenly he sat up and grabbed them. The first letter was from his mother. It described the tremendous relief they all had when it was reported that he was alive and a prisoner of war. This brought home to him how much those at home had suffered and how much they looked forward to his return.

That did it. Now he knew that he must survive and go back to them. So he fought for his life and slowly recovered and eventually got home.

The power in the words of those letters saved his life. This sense of the power of words was very real to the people of the Bible. They believed in the potency of the spoken word. To them it was really alive charged with energy and life. We moderns can understand this when we think of the good or evil that even a few words can do. We in Northern Ireland know this all too well where the wrong words can kill. Even Adolf Hitler knew this all too well. In "Mein Kampf" ("My Struggle"), the book he wrote in 1927, he said: "All great world-shaking events have been brought about not by the written word but by the spoken word."

It is fascinating to look through the Bible and consider the different ways and situations in which God's word came and spoke to different characters. How Isaiah, as a sophisticated city man, had a vision of God's presence in the temple that revolutionised his whole life. Then there was Amos, the country man, quietly minding his flock on the hillside and having time to think. Gradually, as he kept watch, he came to realise all the corruption, injustice and false religion in the land and a burning sense within told him that he had to speak God's word of justice no matter what the cost. Hosea's sense of the reality of God's presence came to him through the tragedy of his own broken marriage. Then Moses at the Burning Bush gets God's call to do something he did not want to do, but he obeys and goes out to lead his people from slavery into a new life. This compelling sense of God's word and call is basic to both Testaments.

But does God's word come to us today? In every age since biblical times there has been that vast procession of those who have heard God's word and answered it. But for the most of us He does not come in visions or dreams but in ordinary everyday events. Albert Schweizer describes in one of his books how the call to medical missionary work in West Africa came to him in a newspaper article. God comes through our listening and thinking, through beauty and goodness, through our inner longings and hopes, through our friends and through strangers, through our needs and fears and so many other unexpected ways.

Why don't we hear him? Is it because we are so busy and preoccupied that we don't have time to think about him? This is how Michel Quoist puts it.

"Goodbye, sir, excuse me, I haven't time".

"I'll come back, I can't wait, I haven't time."

"I must end this letter, I haven't time."

"I'd love to help you but I haven't time."

"I can't accept, I have no time."

"I can't think, I can't read, I'm swamped, I haven't time.

"I'd like to pray, but I haven't time."

I am not asking you tonight, Lord, for time to do this and then that; but your grace to do conscientiously, in the time you give me, what you want me to do.

Love Grandad

DISCOVERING WHO YOU ARE

Dear Chris, This is one of my favourite stories.

It is the story of an African farmer who had spent many years building up his farm.

It was deep in the forest and before he could build anything he had had to clear away the scrub and trees to create a suitable area for setting out buildings and pasture land. Apart from cattle and sheep he specialised in poultry and very quickly collected a large flock of chickens. It took a lot of hard work but after a few years he had it all in good shape. It was set in a long and wide valley surrounded by a range of high mountains and had a wide river winding its way through his land.

One day a visitor arrived at the farm. He explained that he was a naturalist and had come to research this part of the country and asked the farmer if he could look round his farm. To this he readily agreed as indeed he had become very proud of what he had done in creating it. Together they walked round the farm,visiting the stables and byres and the large storage barn. Then they examined the horses and cattle and the crops in the surrounding fields. Finally they came to the chicken run and the farmer noticed that his guest suddenly became very interested, as they stood looking at the birds. Then he exclaimed;

'Do you see that bird there over beside the water pool? It is not a chicken, it's an eagle.''Rubbish', said the farmer. 'It was born a chicken and it will always be a chicken'!

A very lively argument followed and finally the visitor asked the farmer if he could make a test. The farmer agreed but adamantly assured the naturalist that he was wasting his time. 'I know it is a chicken- it was born a chicken and will always be a chicken'!

Together they went over to the birds and caught the suspect. The visitor took the bird in his hand and held it up, so that it could see beyond the chicken run and the other birds, to the open land and beyond to the majestic range of mountains, clear in the blue sky and radiant sunshine.

Slowly he raised his hand with the bird on it and looking at it he said very slowly and firmly:

'Eagle, you are an eagle. You were born for the heavens and not the earth. Stretch forth your wings and fly'.

There was quite a long pause, as the bird looked across the veldt and forest and for a moment lifted its eyes to the mountains. Then it glanced down to where the chickens were pecking for grain among the grass and weeds of the run. Again it paused for a moment and then fluttered out of his hand and quickly raced back to join the others in

the pen. The farmer laughed good humouredly and said to the naturalist.

'Do you see that? The bird's a chicken and will always be a chicken'!

The naturalist replied and asked if he could try again and the farmer agreed confidently. This time he took the bird out of the run across the grass lawn and up the side stairs of the house to the flat roof. Here there was a much wider view of the countryside and the mountains. Once again he held the bird up in his hand, giving it time to take in all the landscape. Then he repeated what he had said earlier:

'Eagle you were born for the heavens and not the earth. Stretch forth your wings and fly'. Once again, as it looked across the country-side it seemed to pause for a moment and then with the corner of its eye it could see the chickens busily pecking at their food and once again it sprang from his hand and fluttering down from the roof raced across to join the chickens.

This time the farmer laughed much louder and said: 'Surely now you can see that the bird is a chicken and always will be'.

The naturalist persisted and asked if he could have one more final chance. To this the farmer readily agreed. This time he took it away from the farm house and the chicken run, on beyond the fields to the open countryside and finally on to higher ground. Here there was a much clearer view of the surrounding countryside and the mountain peaks gleaming in the morning sun. Once again he held it up in his hand and said, 'Eagle, you are an eagle, you were made for the heavens and not the earth. Stretch forth you wings and fly'.

This time the bird lifted its eyes to the majestic outline of the mountains and the piercing rays of the morning sun. At first it remained very still, then it began to quiver and tremble, then suddenly it stretched out its wings and with the great cry of an eagle, rose out of his hand, flew over the nearby forest and then began to soar and soar into the limitless space of the sky towards the rising sun, never to come back!

Love Grandad

FATHER FORGIVE

Dear Chris, This is one of the most unforgettable experiences Granny and I ever had.

In 1985 I was invited to return to Germany where I had been a prisoner of war from 1944-45. I had been attached to Stalag IV A as a YMCA Field Worker and Chaplain. My main task was to visit Work Camps all over the Dresden area. This was late on in the war and many German cities were being attacked by Allied bombers. The climax came on the 13th and 14th of February 1945 when the city was devastated by three Anglo-American Air Raids. Thousands of incendiary bombs had ignited a massive fire storm, raising the temperature to 800-1000 degrees. This caused a mighty suction, as the cool air rushed in to replace the rising hot air. The horrific result was that many people trying to escape from the burning city were sucked back into the inferno. No one knows how many lost their lives and estimates range from 30-100 thousand.

In May 1985 I was invited to go to Germany, as a representative of the British Council of Churches at a gathering of representatives of the different countries that had been involved in the war. The meetings were to take place in Berlin and I agreed to go, on condition that they would arrange for me to revisit Dresden.

That visit will always live in my memory! Our host was Christof Ziemer who was a pastor of the ancient Kreuzkirche, right in the centre of the city and close to the Elbe. It was Rogation Sunday and he invited me to take part in celebrating the eucharist and give a brief sermon. Granny was asked to read the scripture. I had not time to prepare a sermon but just spoke from the heart. I explained how the last time I had been in the city, I had been a prisoner and an enemy. I spoke very frankly about the feelings of my fellow prisoners and how much many of them has suffered with forced marches in the depths of winter. Then I went on to speak of the horrors of the raids and the suffering and death of so many and how saddened and shocked many of the prisoners were by what they had seen.

Finally I spoke of how today we were all gathered round the one Table of our Lord and here received his forgiveness and were able to forgive one another. I concluded with Paul's words:

"For Christ is our peace who has broken down the walls that separate us." I knew that I had been given these words, because I usually have to prepare what I say.

The sequel was later at the beautiful Semper Opera House. The play was 'Die Freischutz' by Karl Von Weber. The last time it had been presented was 40 years earlier on the night of the air raids. During the interval the lady sitting next to Granny began to talk to her. She explained that she had been to the service in the Kreuzkirche with her husband and how much they had been moved by what had taken place. On the night of the raid he had been in barracks, as, at sixteen he was already in the army. Then she described how in the raids his mother, his six year old sister and both his grandparents had been killed. Ever since, he had been filled with hatred and bitterness against the British and Americans and could not forgive. At this point the lights went out and the play continued. When the programme ended, there was a quick exodus and the husband and wife were gone.

Then Granny told me what had happened and what the lady had said and I replied 'I do wish I had had the chance to speak to him'. When we got out on to the street, we were quickly caught up in the large crowds of people hurrying home and I felt very disappointed that I had missed him. Then as we stood there a man came dodging between the cars and pushing his way through the people. He rushed up to me and grasped my hand. I could see that there were tears in his eyes and he simply said 'Now I can forgive' He wrung my hand and disappeared into the crowd and I never saw him again.

I believe that there is a rediscovery of the Christian message of forgiveness. Think of how central it is in the story of Christ. In the prayer he taught us to pray: "Forgive us... as we forgive". Then on the Cross he prayed "Father forgive them".

We in Corrymeela cherish our link with Coventry Cathedral through their "Cross of Nails Community". The story of the marvellous 20th Century building, springing from the war devastated ruins of the ancient 12th Century building is a living parable for today of life through death. But for me the outstanding memory is not of the modern building, but rather of the simple altar that stands within the broken walls and roofless sanctuary of the old building.

On this altar stands a fire charred wooden cross. Two beams had been rescued from the ruins and someone had put one of the beams across and formed a cross. This had been placed on the altar and above it inscribed simply: "FATHER FORGIVE". Is there any more important word for us today in Ireland and across our world?

Love Grandad

ON SEEING THE OTHER SIDE!

Dear Chris, I believe you've been with your Dad to watch a football match at Windsor Park in Belfast.

Some time ago two young men went to Windsor Park to watch a football match. When they came to the admission turnstile the first man put down just half the admission fee. When the attendant asked why, he replied: "Well I'm blind in one eye and will only be able to see half the match". Then his friend's turn came and he also put down just half the fee. "Well, what's wrong with you?" the attendant asked. "Oh I've only come to watch one team". There is no record of what the attendant muttered in reply.

But surely that is just the trouble in our little country. We have been content for so long to follow one side and consider only one point of view and ignore the other. We have become accustomed to a very selective attitude to life. This is how a famous Ulster man, Sir Tyrone Guthrie, once put it: "We were born apart, we lived apart, we prayed apart, we never learned to come together. There was no institution that made it possible." This selective approach is also shown in how we so often stereotype each other. That is the habit of putting people into categories and classes and so being unable to see them as real people.

Sometimes the young adult groups that come to Corrymeela do "role playing" as part of their programme. In an improvised situation or drama the Protestant tries to play the part of a Catholic and the Catholic that of a Protestant. Through this many have come to understand in a new way the other point of view. In the process each participant is able to see the other person in a new way and usually to discover how close they are to one another.

A number of years ago Corrymeela organised the visit of four school groups of 12 year old children from Belfast, two being Catholic and two Protestant. The official programme was field work in local geography and it lasted for five days. It turned out to be a great success and when the young people got back, one of them came to my home in Belfast and pleaded with me to arrange for them to go back for another stay with the same people. I will never forget what he said to me. "At the start we were all scared and afraid that there would be a lot of arguments and fighting. But it wasn't like that at all. We discovered that they were just like us". That to us in Corrymeela has been not only an unforgettable sign of hope but also an unceasing challenge to us to enable people both young and old to meet together and rediscover what they have in common - indeed to discover each other.

For centuries our churches have been apart. There was the family split up at the Reformation. But now the process of rediscovering each other is taking place and the wonderful realisation that we are brothers and sisters and belong together. Of course there are differences that have to be faced but the things we hold in common are far greater than those that hold us apart. And for us all Christ is at the centre, and the closer we come to him, the closer we come to each other.

Love Grandad

THE GIFT OF THE GAB

Dear Chris, I don't think any of us in our family are ever stuck for words. In fact we all have the 'gift of the gab'.

One of the great gifts that people of this island share is the remarkable ability to express themselves with eloquence and humour. But every day brings home to us the potential of words for good or evil. The apostle James was right on the mark when he wrote "Even so the tongue is a little member but boasteth of great things".

Speech is one of the supreme endowments we have been given. It is the foundation of all our relationships and a basic part of our humanity. We all have learnt in these difficult days in the history of our country to understand the importance of what is said or written by the Press, the Media, Politicians and Community leaders and indeed our own everyday conversation. This is a very subtle question, not only about words, but when, where and how they are used. There are several ways in which we can use our tongues.

First of all there are bad sorts of words. Those that are sectarian, abusive, emotive, vulgar, negative, threatening and exaggerated. A study of many graffiti on Belfast gable walls and elsewhere will provide ample illustration of the misuse of language in this way.

Then the bad use of good words. So easy to engage in rumour and gossip, to complain and criticise, to be negative and pessimistic.

There also can be good words at the right time. It is important to see that every word, every conversation and every discussion can help or hinder the search for peace and reconciliation. One of the most valuable things that we can do is in the everyday contacts we have and the values and attitudes we present. It is through such things that change in thinking can take place. For it is in this way that, as James Hilton wrote, "the private opinions of today become the public opinions of tomorrow."

The importance of having the right word at the right time reminds me of May 8th 1945 - my last day of captivity and the first of freedom. But it was a nerve-shattering day for me and my friends. It was May and the weather was very warm and we were uncertain where to go. Eventually some 20 of us took off on our own in an attempt to get through. After several days on the road we arrived in a town called Teplitz where a very fierce battle had just taken place between the Red Army and a fanatical Hermann Goering division making their last stand. Very fortunately for us our arrival coincided with the end of the battle and we were very relieved to see large white sheets hanging out of the house windows in surrender although spasmodic firing continued.

It was a very tense and frightening experience and a situation of great uncertainty. We rested for a time on the edge of the town and decided that our best course of action was to contact the Russians. We were very unsure as to what reception we would get, as everything was very fluid and chaotic. But we knew we had to make a move. Then we saw them. They were certainly a tough battle scarred group of men, very heavily armed with all types of automatic weapons. As we approached them, we wondered what they would do and if they would know that we were prisoners. Then as we came up to them, one of our party shouted out, "Tovarich-Kamarad". Suddenly they seemed to get the message and broad smiles spread across their faces. They relaxed and put aside their weapons, warmly embraced us and wrung our hands and offered us wine and biscuits. Then finally with many friendly gestures they directed us to the Allied lines. It certainly proved to be a right word at the right time.

Love Grandad

THE STORY OF CHRISTOPHER

Dear Christopher, I thought you would like to have this story about the meaning of your name.

Once upon a time there lived in the Far East a giant of enormous size and strength. Indeed, he was bigger than Goliath. Offero was his name. One day he set out to find a Master, for though he was willing to serve yet he was very proud and would not serve a Master who was not stronger than himself. Then he found a strong King whom all the World obeyed, who was Master of great armies and who seemed to be afraid of no one. So he agreed to serve him.

But one day the name of the Devil was mentioned in the King's hearing and Offero noticed that the King was afraid. Then he knew then that the devil must be stronger and mightier than this King, so he forsook the King and entered the Devil's service.

For a time he was content to serve him, for he thought he was serving the strongest Master in the world. But one day when he was following the Devil, they came to a Cross and Offero noticed that when the Devil saw it, he trembled and turned back. This seemed odd, so Offero questioned the Devil and found out that he was afraid of Jesus, the Son of God who had died on the Cross to save the world, and then had risen and gone to Heaven. So Offero saw that He was stronger than the Devil, so Offero said at once, "I will serve you no longer, I will serve Jesus"

But he did not find it very easy. He fell in with a good hermit who served Jesus. He tried to teach Offero to read the Bible, but the poor giant found that he could not master even the ABC and very simple words. Then he tried another way, to pray and fast like the hermit. But fasting did not suit his gigantic body and his huge muscles. Was there no other way in which he could serve his new Master? He discovered that there was a river near by, with deep water and raging floods. The ford or crossing place was here and it was very treacherous and dangerous. It was here for the love of Christ that he was determined to spend his time. Here beside the river he built his hut and he was so big and strong that he was able to carry many travellers across on his great shoulders.

One very wild night, as he sat in his little hut by the fire, he heard the roar of the wind and the lash of the rain and he thought to himself, surely no one would want to cross the river that night.

But just as he was settling down for the night, a knock, very gentle and soft, fell on his door. Wondering who would want to cross on such a night, he opened the door and there stood a child, a little boy, and he wanted very much to cross. So he agreed, though he knew it was very dangerous and that they both could easily be swept away by the flood.

He gently took the little boy on his great strong shoulders and started to fight his way through the torrent. At first the child seemed as light as a feather to Offero, but as they got down into the deeper water his burden seemed to grow greater and greater. Then a great struggle began, as the force and depth of the stream almost knocked him off his feet.

Sometimes the water passed over his head but he fought on and on until at last his foothold became firmer and surer and he knew he had won through.

Then stepping out on to the bank, he set his burden down. He looked at it in surprise and discovered that what he had thought was a little child, was in fact a fully grown man. but such a man he had never seen before! At once he knew that it was Christ whom he had tried to serve and bowing down he worshipped him. Ever since then Offero has been known as Christopher - the one who carried Christ.

Of course this was just a legend but it is very true to life and a very challenging thought. We find Christ only as we serve others. Think of Christ's own words: "In so far as you did it to one of these brothers of mine you did it to me. For when I was hungry you fed me, thirsty you gave me drink. when I was a stranger you entertained me, when unclothed, you clothed me. When I was ill you looked after me. When in prison, you visited me".

Love Grandad

WHAT IS FREEDOM?

Dear Chris, You know that I was a prisoner in World War II.

Let me tell you about a man who was a prisoner with me in a camp near Dresden. This man was from England and he was a doctor. He had been captured in Greece and had been three years in captivity. I saw quite a lot of him and almost every time we got into conversation he would be complaining. Sometimes it was about the conditions we lived in or the Germans or the food or the other prisoners and how miserable they were. Then he would say "If only I could get away from here and back home, how different it would be." Well it so happened that he applied for repatriation and eventually this was granted and in a few weeks he was sent back to England and home.

You can guess our surprise when a few months later we received a letter from him in England. We were all very amazed by what he wrote. He told us of how bored he was at being back home and how much he wished he was back in the camp and how greatly he missed the companionship.

His letter made us in the prison camp understand that freedom is much more than just freedom from physical confinement and that there are very many other ways in which we can be shut in apart from barbed wire and high walls. No matter how much we try, we cannot get away from ourselves, our thoughts, our feelings, our fears, our achieve-ments and disappointments, our pleasures and pains. The all important thing is how we respond to these things that happen to us and affect our lives. So it is our responsibility to decide whether we will let what happens to us imprison us or give us freedom.

It is amazing to consider the different things that can imprison us. I'm not just thinking about obvious situations such as alcoholism, drug addiction or compulsive gambling, but rather of mental attitudes or should I say complexes. And if they are not faced and exposed they can totally master a person's life.

For example there are those people who always want to dominate, to hold the limelight. His or her ideas must be accepted. Such people find it almost impossible to listen. They'll resign if their suggestions are not accepted. Think of the devastation such people create at every level of society. Another baneful attitude that can imprison is resentment. Think of some slight or misunderstanding and how it can escalate if it is not faced. Often you will hear people say when you mention a mutual acquaintance, "Oh, we have not spoken for years." Some difference of opinion has been allowed to develop and to break up a relationship. Or a grudge that can develop into an obsession. I remember a school master who felt that he had been unfairly treated in the way of promotion. As time passed, it became a deep resentment and coloured all his life and his relationships.

Perhaps for us in Ireland the most potent and insidious chain is prejudice, because it can so easily develop into bitterness, hate and indeed violence. Prejudice is to pre-judge people by labelling them and putting them into categories and so being blind to the person behind the label. Recently I asked Helen Lewis, who had been in the Auschwitz Concentration Camp during the war, why she did not hate. She replied: "To hate is self destructive." Hopefully there will soon be a political settlement but if it is to last, the terrible chains of prejudice and hatred have to be broken.

The very popular Belfast comedian, the late James Young, in his hilarious monologues used to exhort his audience with the phrase "Catch yourselves on." I am sure he was right. I always like to go back to Jesus' story of the Prodigal son. How the younger son left home and went into the far country "to do his own thing," as we would say. He had a very lively time in the far country, until he became broke without a penny. Then there is that amazing phrase: "He came to himself." What did it mean? It meant that for the first time in his life he "caught himself on." He discovered who he really was, where he belonged and the place he had in his home and what his destiny was.

This is what St Augustine wrote when he looked back on his own very similar experience: "You have made us for yourself and our hearts are restless until they find their rest in you."

Love Grandad

AGAPE

Dear Kate, This is a very important letter because it is really the heart and soul of what life is about.

There is a story told about the Evangelist St.John, the man who wrote "God is love... if any man tells me that he loves God whom he does not see but does not love his brother whom he does see, he simply is a liar." It is of this John that the story is told that, in the evening of his long life, he would sit for hours with his young disciples gathered round his feet. One day, as it is related in this well established tradition, one of his disciples complained: "John, you always talk about love, about God's love for us and about our love for one another. Why don't you tell us about something else besides love?" The disciple who had once, as a youth, laid his head over the heart of God made man, is said to have replied, "Because there is nothing else, just love... love... love!

One of the most important and necessary starting points in talking about Agape or Christian Love is to be clear in our minds what it means. Often the word 'love' seems to be like a great umbrella under which several different ideas shelter. Some people associate it with what is soft and sentimental with a supreme emphasis on feelings. Of course feelings are important but they are only a part of something that embraces every part of life. Think of how Jesus replied when He was asked which was the greatest commandment: "You shall love the Lord your God with all your heart, with all your soul and with all your mind. This is the great and first commandment." Then He continued, "And the second is like it, you shall love your neighbour as yourself."

The great central affirmation is "God is love." This is where it all begins. As I write, I ask myself has this just become a piece of religious jargon or a platitude, something that we don't really grasp and absorb. Yet I believe that our whole faith stands or falls with the truth or falsehood of this phrase. Is this really true and do we really believe it? When we read the Bible it recurs again and again like the theme that runs through a Beethoven Symphony. We can't avoid seeing it. "God is love," "God so loved the world ..." And it is this love of God for us that is the foundation and power of all our love. "A new commandment I give to you that you love one another." "By this shall you know that you are my disciples because you love one another." "We love him... because he first loved us."

If we believe that God is love, we have grasped what is the most important and amazing fact in all history and human experience. It gives us a new perspective and motivation in our everyday living. And far more, it gives us a profound hope and anticipation, as we look into the future. If God is love, He cannot live in isolation. Love, if it is real, must have someone to love and someone to love it.

This is how James Weldon Johnston the Negro Poet puts it:

'And God stepped out on space and He looked around and said,
"I'm lonely... I'll make me a world."
And God looked around on all he had made,
And God said, "I'm lonely still."
And the great God Almighty who lit the sun and fixed it in the heavens
Who flung the stars to the far corners of the night,
Who rounded the earth in the middle of His hand,-

This Great God, like a mammy bending over her baby,
Kneeling down in the dust, toiling over a lump of clay
Till He shaped it in His own image:
Then into it He blew the breath of life,
And man became a living soul.'

The love of Christ is not cheap or easy. It is radical and costly. It means that you stop thinking just about yourself but of others. It means that the focus of your life turns out to others instead of in to self. It means, as Jesus said, "Losing your life to find it."

I have seen the love of Christ in so many places and been shown it in so many different ways:

I think of the youth leader who gives himself in supporting and encouraging a group of unemployed young adults.

Of the mother who studied Braille in order to help her blind son in his education.

Of those who give their time and energy to support families of prisoners or families who have lost loved ones in the violence.

Of those who regularly raise money to support Tear Fund or Christian Aid or other agencies.

Of young people who go out and work in Third World countries.

Of those who give their time in organising and running holidays for families who could not afford to go away.

Of the parents who give unlimited love and care to their handicapped child.

'Then the king will say to those on his right hand, "You have my Father's blessing; come and enter and possess the kingdom that has been ready for you since the world was made.

For when I was hungry you gave me food,
When thirsty, you gave me drink,
When I was a stranger you took me into your home,
When naked you clothed me

When I was ill you came to my help
When in prison you visited me
I tell you this: anything you did for one of my brothers here, however humble, you did it for me."'

Love Grandad

THE KINGDOM IS WITHIN YOU

Dear Kate, Though this letter was written in 1515, it is really timeless and one that inspires us to awaken to the beauty and joy in life.

An old priest wrote it to a young friend, a great lady, on Christmas Eve, 1515. He has left no other name than Brother John.

To the Most Illustrious Countess Allagia Aldobrandeschi on the Via del Martelli, Florence.

Most Noble Contessina,

I salute you. Believe me your most devoted friend. The rascal who carries this letter, if he devour them not on the way, will crave our acceptance of some of the fruits of our garden. Would that the peace of Heaven might reach you through such things of earth.

Contessina, forgive an old man's babble. But I am your friend and my love for you goes deep. There is nothing I can give you which you have not got but there is much, very much, that, while I cannot take it, you can take. No Heaven can come to us unless our hearts find rest in it today. Take Heaven. No peace in the future which is not hidden in this present little instant. Take peace.

The gloom of the world is but a shadow. Behind it, yet within your reach, is joy. There is radiance and glory in the darkness, could we but see; and to see, we have only to look. Contessina, I beseech you to look.

Life is so generous a giver, but we, judging its gifts by their covering, cast them away as ugly or heavy or hard. Remove the covering and you will find beneath it a living splendour, woven in love, by wisdom with power. Welcome it. Grasp it, and you touch the Angel's hand that brings it to you. Everything we call a trial, a sorrow or a duty believe that Angel's hand is there; the gift is there and the wonder of the overshadowing Presence. Our joys too, be not content with them as joys. They too conceal diviner gifts.

Life is full of meaning and purpose, so full of beauty beneath its covering, that you will find that earth but cloaks your heaven. Courage then to claim it: that is all. But courage you have and the knowledge that we are pilgrims together, wending through unknown country, home.

And so, at this Christmas time, I greet you: not quite as the world sends greeting but with profound esteem and with the prayer that for you now and forever, the day breaks and the shadows flee away.

I have the honour to be your friend, though the least worthy of them. Fra Giovanni.

Love Grandad

RELIGION AND SPORT

Dear Kate, I'm so glad to know that you are keen on athletics, net-ball and lacrosse. Sport is a great preparation for life.

My memory often goes back to the days when I played rugby at school. I can remember some of the matches we played, the schools we visited and the amount of training we did, not only to keep fit but at the same time to try to master the various skills that were needed such as passing, tackling, defending and all the other things that are important, if the game is to be played well.

One year I managed to get a place on the 1st Fifteen of my school. Of course I was very keen and did a lot of training and practice. My position was Full-Back, the last line of defence and it needed a lot of skills and I had to train very hard. At that time there was a well known retired doctor who was a very keen supporter of the school team. Just after I got my place on the team, he invited me round to his house to talk about rugby. He was recognised as a leading authority on the game.

After we had talked for some time, he turned to me sharply and almost roared, "What is the first rule for Full-Back play?" I wasn't sure what he meant. After a pause he roared, "Never let the ball bounce." Then he continued, "What is the second rule for Full-Back play?" Then again he roared, "Never let the ball bounce." A third time the question came followed by the same answer, "Never let the ball bounce."

That was good advice which I never forgot. Remember that a rugby ball is oval and when it bounces it can go in any direction. A great many tries or scores result from a lucky or unlucky bounce of the ball. I discovered a very important thing that if I was really determined, I would catch almost every ball before it hit the ground and bounced. But in order to do so I had to be really determined to get to the ball and catch it. That sort of determination can win matches.

I have learned many things playing various games that apply much wider in life. And this is specially true in our religion. If you want your faith to be real and alive you've got to be determined about it. I am sure the reason many young people get "turned off" from religion is that so often they don't really take it seriously like the player who never trains, is rather hazy about the rules and only turns out when it suits him. They want it the easy way and refuse to understand that with anything in life that is really worthwhile, effort is required, time is essential and thought irreplaceable. Many people would like it to be otherwise. They want religion but at cut cost prices.

Love Grandad

THE FORGOTTEN FACTOR

Dear Kate, This story is one I specially like. To me it is the centre and core of religion - that God is Love.

I read a rather whimsical description of Hell some time ago. It started with a very vivid account of a really lush golf course. It was laid out on an idyllic site close to a lovely coast line and, of course, convenient to the city. The greens were beautifully constructed and perfectly manicured. The velvet fairways were lined with evergreen trees. Even the bunkers seemed to be player-friendly and altogether even the so-called 'rough' presented few hazards or threats.

Our golfer emerges from the magnificently appointed club house and has easy access to the first tee. His loaded club trolley is in the care of a well groomed caddie. The golfer is immaculately turned out with studded shoes, colourful slacks and a matching shirt. A silk scarf adorns his neck and a smart long peaked cap protects his eyes.

It is an ideal day for the game with the blue sea twinkling in the sun across the sand dunes and a very pleasant breeze gently wafting down the course. As they approach the first tee the caddie pulls out the driver and passes it to the golfer who is eagerly scanning the fairway and the distant flag, gently flapping from the hole of his target, the first green.

Then suddenly the whole scene dramatically changes. The caddie goes to the bag of clubs and to his utter horror discovers that there are no golf balls in it. The remarks of the player were inaudible because of the wind and the caddie beats a hasty retreat to the club house. The whole purpose and point of the game is lost, because there is nothing to play with. The central item that made the game possible is missing.

This is a parable of the real world, of what happens when the true and overall purpose is lost or forgotten. Deep down inside we know that the most important and real thing in life is love and all those things that express and nourish it such as our relationships, our friends, our homes, community, - in a word, all those things that make up the fabric of our everyday lives, all that makes life really meaningful and that sustains us in difficult times and which we can celebrate when life is good.

But this is what the life and teaching of Jesus was all about. Again and again he tells us that God is love, that he loves the world, and, indeed, that love is the key to the problems and challenges of our times. He tells us that the distinguishing mark of his followers is that they love one another. "God is love" is the core definition given in the Bible. That is the meaning and purpose and heart of all our living.

Today much of our current culture runs against this way of thinking which is based on self-giving. It fosters care and concern for ourselves and our interests before anything else. The key question to ask is "What's in this for me?" If there is anything that you may query, there is the response, "Don't be soft, remember business is business." Of course this philosophy of life can be expressed in the most persuasive way with all the power of modern technology, ubiquitous advertising both normal and subliminal and with incessant media pressure in every home in the country. It can all be presented in such plausible language and there is all the expertise to manipulate.

Kenneth Graham's "Wind in the Willows" portrays this outlook in the draft programme of the concert Toad of Toad Hall plans to organise:

SPEECH..................................by Toad
(There will be other speeches by Toad during the evening)
ADDRESS.................................by Toad
Song......................................by Toad
(composed by himself)
OTHER COMPOSITIONS...................by Toad
(will be sung in the course of the evening by the composer)

This is the choice we all are making all the time - whether we live for ourselves or for others. The same challenge was issued away back in 1260 BC by Moses, as he made his final speech to his people, as they were about to enter the Promised Land:

This day...I have set before you life and death, blessings and curses. Now choose life that you and your children may live and that you may love the Lord your God, listen to his voice, and hold fast to him.

Many centuries later the apostle Paul sums it all up for us:

"And now I will show you the most excellent way. If I speak in the tongues of men and of angels, but have not love, I am only a resounding gong or a clanging cymbal. If I have the gift of prophecy and can fathom all mysteries and all knowledge, and if I have a faith that can move mountains, but have not love, I am nothing. If I give all I possess to the poor and surrender my body to the flames, but have not love, I am nothing...

And now these three remain: faith, hope and love. But the greatest of these is love.

Love Grandad

THE ITALIAN COLONEL

Dear Kate, This letter describes one of the toughest experiences of my life and the inspiring good will of the ordinary Italian people.

I will never forget the 30th July, 1942 when with several hundred British and South African prisoners of war, captured in North Africa, we arrived in our cattle wagons at the ancient city of Lucca in Tuscany. Though we had been prisoners for barely six weeks, we had been moved from one transit camp to another, some five altogether. Now our hopes were high that this would be a more permanent home. Our camp was several miles from Lucca, as we discovered, when finally our train stopped at a small station out in the middle of the country. We had to walk for quite a distance, eagerly scanning the horizon for our new home. When we did at last locate it, we were somewhat deflated. We identified it by the massive barbed-wired perimeter fence with huge arc-lights that ringed the area like a greyhound track with tall sentry boxes placed at regular intervals round the wire.

The camp was on a gentle slope. At the top several wooden huts provided accommodation for the camp administration and the Italian soldiers who were responsible for security. There were no other buildings otherwise and the lower part of the site was bisected by several stagnant streams. And we all began to speculate just where our accommodation would be. The mystery was quickly solved. Our hosts began to distribute small bivvy tents – one for each six prisoners. These we erected ourselves.

Mod cons were similarly primitive with long trenches and a thin wooden bench to sit on. Washing facilities were no better with several water taps and a stack of tin basins. Rations turned out to be equally basic and it was a new experience for us to experience real hunger. No Red Cross food arrived for several weeks and when it did come there was usually only one parcel for seven men. In addition the Italians insisted that every tin should be punctured in case we might hoard the food and be tempted to try to escape.

In contrast to these sordid conditions there were the incredible stretch of marvellous scenery all around us. Looking north we had a lovely glimpse of the little village on the slopes of Monte Pisone. The small white houses ringed round the hill and between them were terraces of vines and olive groves. Away to the east the open country was spread out like a patch-work quilt with green and golden fields, reminding me of a Van Gogh print. Then far away in the distance the massive outline of the Apennines, the spinal cord of Italy. What a relief to the squalor and incessant noise of our overcrowded patch to be able

to look away across the land and contemplate majestic mountains.

I have one very special memory of those grim days. My YMCA colleague, Harold Barker, could speak fluent French and he was asked by the Italian Colonel who was in charge of the camp to act as his interpreter. In civilian life he had been a village solicitor and like so many other Italians had been forced to enlist in the army. One day he offered to take Harold for a walk outside the camp and suggested that he might bring two other prisoners with him. So Captain Hill, a young Salvation Army officer, and myself made up the party. Few experiences have thrilled me more than that short walk. How exhilarating to get away from the sordid overcrowded camp enclosure! How soothing it was to see ordinary Italians at work on their land. Here, we thought, was the other side of this sad country that would live on when Fascism and Mussolini would be forgotten. As we listened to the Colonel we could see that he also was a victim of the war. He had fought with the Allies in the First World War. He hated all war but like so many others he had had no choice and had to enlist in the army. His sole ambition now was to return to his home, his wife and family.

I recall that the Colonel had a great desire to learn English and on the walk he tried to converse with us, using the few phrases he knew.. It was quite exhausting trying to converse with him, to understand what he was trying to say and make a sensible reply. Fortunately early on I discovered one thing - he loved proverbs. So whenever I became ex-hausted trying to understand what he was trying to say, I would give him a proverb such as "All roads lead to Rome " or "When in Rome do as the Romans do". This latter sent him into chuckles of laughter and kept him content and occupied until we got back to the camp. Anyway the walk took us up to Pisonia, the lovely little village on the hill. As we climbed up to it we could see the small white houses and the inhabitants coming out to stare at us.

As we approached them I began to speculate what sort of a reception they would give us. Would they ignore us or would they be hostile and perhaps abuse us. After all we were the enemy!

How wrong I was! True at first they stood their ground and stared at us. Then suddenly it all began to happen when one woman came across to us with a bunch of flowers. That started a real procession of gift-bearers. They came from all directions with grapes, figs, tomatoes, plums dates, peaches and oranges. We were very deeply touched and responded as best we could with our very limited Italian phrase "Grazio Molto". Their very warm smiles assured us that they had got the message.

Even after so many years I can still remember the great lift that simple encounter with those Italian villagers gave to us and how it lifted our spirits at a very crucial time. It stayed with us through all the ardours of the three years that lay ahead of us in captivity. Indeed it was much more – it was an annunciation of hope for the future and also a challenge to make the best use of the time before us and to accept the opportunity of supporting and encouraging those who found the conditions overwhelming. No matter what happened there was that constant sense that there was a real job to be done and that this was where God wanted us to be and somehow that awareness made all the difference.

Many years later at Corrymeela we would sing a song at worship that always carried me back to that camp in Lucca.

You shall cross the barren desert
But you shall not die of thirst,
You will wander far from safety,
Though you do not know the way.
You shall speak your words to foreign men
And they shall understand.
You shall see the face of God and live;
Be not afraid
I go before you always;
Come follow me,
And I will give you rest.

Love Grandad

WHAT A WONDERFUL WORLD

Dear Kate, I wonder if you know that well known song 'O What a wonderful world?'

Of course, that was the title of that marvellous number that Louis Armstrong, the famous Afro-American singer, made so very much his own and so famous. Let me remind you of some of the lines:

I see trees of green
Red roses too
I see them bloom
For me and you
And I think to myself
What a wonderful world

I see skies of blue
And clouds of white
The blessed day
The sacred night
And I think to myself
What a wonderful world.

As I listen to it sung in Louis' inimitable style, it moves me. It is a beautiful and indeed passionate affirmation of the glory and wonder of this world which we inhabit and which at times we take so much for granted and even ignore.

Whenever I listen to Louis Armstrong's lyric, my thoughts go away back to my student days at Queen's, when I took part in a Field Week, studying the geology of Ballycastle and district. It was during the Easter holidays and the sharp bright weather was ideal for the trips we made on foot each day. Professor Jack Charlesworth was not only an eminent geologist but also an excellent teacher and the excursions we made each day took us to many fascinating places. I will never forget our trip to Fair Head past Loughareema with its man made island or crannoch. What a panorama we had of the highlands and islands of the ancient kingdom of Dalriada which links Ireland and Scotland. Then those mighty basaltic columns rising together five hundred feet and somehow dominating the Moyle Water and also being the most northerly point in Ireland.

Space will not allow me to describe the Vanishing Lake, the North Star Dyke and of course, the Giant's Causeway with its wonderful natural architecture.

Then there was the awareness of the time factor how these headlands, mountains, rocks, beaches and seas were created more than four and a half million years ago. There is the sheer wonder and delight its beauty radiates today. We contemplate on all the forces that have shaped it: the glaciers, earthquakes and volcanic action. Again there is the ever present movement of the sea with its different moods and changing patterns.

Of course this is only a small part of the story of creation, as there is also the amazing story of man's creation.

Can we really believe with some people that this all happened by chance? Is the whole created order and man himself just 'a chance accident in a back water' or 'a chance collocation of atoms' - not a very complimentary description to say the least! It reminds me of the parody written of the children's hymn 'Twinkle, twinkle little star'

'Twinkle, twinkle little star
We know exactly what you are
You're just combusting so much mass
O, C, and N and Hydrogen gas'.

Or again there is the great misfortune that we can live unaware of all the marvel and glory of creation and life. The Victorian poetess, Elizabeth Barratt Browning warns us:

'Earth's crammed with heaven...
But only he who sees, takes off his shoes'.

I am sure that this was what Christ meant when he said 'Except you become as little children, you shall not enter the Kingdom of Heaven'. I began to understand how true this was when I read these lines that Granny had written after she had been for a walk with Christopher, our eight year old grandson, on the beach in Donegal.

"Granny
See this basket of shells,
I picked up from the beach?
Here are shiny black mussels
There are 'butterflies' wings
Lets make a shell picture"
"Granny,
Look at these wild flowers
I picked on the lane.
Buttercups, daisies, yellow and white,
Thistles and harebells, purple and blue
Let's press them and make a flower picture"
"Granny,
Look up - the stars have come out
The clouds have rolled back
And the sky is all twinkling with candles
It's not dark any more

Don't you think
That we live
In a wonderful world?"
Wasn't he just saying what a poet wrote some 3000 years ago:
"The heavens declare the glory of God and the firmament showeth His handiwork?"

Love Grandad

BE YOUR AGE

Dear Patrick, Living here in Northern Ireland you'll know exactly what I am saying in this letter.

Have you ever heard of the Axolotl? It has been described as "the most famous of amphibia." It is a native of Mexico. Here, in waters abundant in food and always warm, it lives contentedly, a tadpole with true gills but it refuses to take the plunge into maturity. It is born a tadpole, it lives as a tadpole and it becomes the parent of other axolotls, all without growing up. Then someone decided to experiment. Some specimens were taken away in a tank to Paris, and there, in the colder water and different food they suddenly transformed themselves into the next generation and turned out all the time to be the larvae of salamanders.

At home in the warm water they did not trouble to grow up and had even learnt how to reproduce their kind while still infants. Theirs was a case of arrested development - they refused to 'grow up'.

What would you think of the builder who kept on working at the foundations or the student at the University who never stopped talking about his A Levels or the musician who only played the scales or the doctor who only talked about anatomy and physiology? One of the saddest things in life is when people refuse to grow up, when they stop developing mentally and emotionally. They refuse to think or listen or learn. They just want to stay as they are and be left alone. They want to live the Lotus leaf existence and give up the journey.

To live is to be open to change - to be willing to move on. Here indeed "we have no abiding city". The law of life is about movement, growth, change and growing up. It is interesting to note how much time and space in the media and popular literature is devoted to the world of travel and exploration. Most of us are fascinated to read about journeys, pilgrimages, Illiads and Odysseys. This is because we identify with this sense of being on the move. It touches something deep in us. Each one of us is aware that we are on our own journey and have to adjust to it by growing and changing in ourselves. But there is always the temptation to stay as we are.

What about the Axolotl in us? What are the things that keep us from growing? This is very important for us who live in Northern Ireland. What are the things that make change so difficult?

We all have a choice to make in whether we live by fear or by faith.

Fear is a negative way. It thrives on rumour, half-truth and lies. It flourishes in the dim atmosphere of mythology and fanaticism, it is kept alive by set opinions and closed minds. It is maintained and reinforced

by:
   Refusal to think for oneself.
   Refusal to listen to the other person and the other point of view.
   Refusal to scrutinise our own attitudes.
   Refusal to examine new possibilities and ways of working together.

   Faith is to be willing to venture and take risks.
   It is willingness to listen and talk together.
   It is the willingness to do all the little and big things that are possible in political, social and religious life to foster trust.
   It is the willingness to follow the call of Christ - "Blessed are the peace makers."
   It is an unqualified call to grow up in our faith and commitment;
   We do well to take St Paul's advice:
   "Let us leave behind the elementary teaching about Christ and go forward to adult understanding. Let us not lay over and over again the foundation truths... no, if God allows us, let us go on."

Love Grandad

THE CULTURE OF PEACE

Dear Patrick, This is what I said at the opening of the new house at Corrymeela in June 1998.

It is with a deep sense of gratitude that we meet here today to declare this building open. There is so much that we are thankful for. Indeed time would not be adequate to mention all those who have made this day possible. We acknowledge and thank them.

Today I cannot but recall that time almost 33 years ago when some of us gathered very close to where we are now. We affirmed our faith in the reconciling power of God and proclaimed our vision for this place that "it would come to be known as the Open Village - open to all of goodwill who were willing to meet each other, learn from each other and work together for the good of all."

At this time it is chastening and inspiring to acknowledge that our prayer was answered and so much of our vision fulfilled.We can relate to the surprise of the Patriarch Jacob who said after his vision, "Surely God was in this place though I knew it not." But today we cannot but remember the way we have come - the unfinished journey we still make or the exodus from the old ways to the new. We live in a country that loves symbols. Alas, they have often been negative and provocative.

But today we offer this new House as a living and positive symbol of that new society that we have longed for, prayed and striven for over so many bleak years; a role model, a trailer of that society that is coming into being. We offer it today, because we have learned that it works. Today we are deeply inspired and encouraged by the affirmation of the Agreement and we salute our political leaders for their courage and commitment. But we know, as they know, that we are only at the start, as we enter a new stage in the process. And, we know that the buck stops with each one of us.

What then is our task? It is surely how we move from the culture of violence to the culture of peace. That is the challenge each one of us faces. After all, our culture embraces the whole of our lives: how we think, how we relate to each other and how we treat each other. That is your responsibility and mine. No longer can we scapegoat our politicians.

There is something else that must be said. If the culture of peace is to flourish and take root, we must create a culture of forgiveness. We do well to listen to the advice of Nelson Mandela:

"No man is born hating another person. People must learn to hate and if they can learn to hate they can learn to love."

And one greater than Mandela has bidden us, in the best known prayer ever prayed:

"Forgive us as we forgive those who sin against us."

Our longings and prayers are summed up for us in Seamus Heaney's lines:

History says, Don't hope
On this side of the grave.
But then, once in a lifetime
The longed for tidal wave
Of justice can rise up,
And hope and history rhyme.

So hope for a great change
On the far side of revenge
Believe that a further shore
Is reachable from here.

Love Grandad

PLOTZENSEE

Dear Patrick, This visit to Plotzensee remains as a perpetual reminder of those who were prepared to stand against the tide of Nazi-
ism, no matter what the cost.

A few years ago I was invited to Spandau in Berlin to take part in an
ecumenical conference and tell about the work of Corrymeela. We were
visually reminded of the divided Germany every time we looked out of
the window, as the massive Berlin Wall dominated the outlook. There
was, however, another experience that made a much deeper impression
on me.

One of the Pastors agreed to show me round the district and the first
place we visited was the Plotzensee Prison. The object of the visit was
a small red-brick outhouse within the grounds of the prison. We were
told that this was used by the Nazis as an execution chamber from 1933-
1945. It looked very much like an old and rather dilapidated school-
room. It was a rectangular room about 24 by 12 feet. The only light
came through two long arched windows. We looked round and at first in
the gloomy light the room seemed empty, but as our eyes adjusted to
the dimness we could see that it was not bare. It was, in fact, an
execution chamber and was divided from two other rooms by a large
black curtain. Behind this on the left was a wash basin and on the right
stood a guillotine. As we slowly took this in we then saw a massive iron
beam running across the ceiling from wall to wall. This bar held eight
strong hooks to facilitate rapid hanging, an alternative to the guillotine.
We were told that "executions were carried out in rapid succession and
all the victims met death with complete calm; they showed no fear and
maintained their dignity to the last."

As Prussian Minister of the Interior, Hermann Goering said "The
measures I take will not be inhibited by any legal considerations... my
job is not to administer justice but only to destroy and exterminate,
nothing more."

So here in this small dingy room from 1933-1945 - 2,800 men and
women were hung with wires to the hooks, while others were
guillotined. Included were men and women from many different
backgrounds and nations. There were politicians, diplomats, clergy,
academics, trade unionists, soldiers, workers and journalists.

This is not a pleasant letter to write. But it is important for all of us
to remember that such things did happen and they happened in this
century. It is even more important to remember with respect and
honour the multitudes of men and women who, when the ultimate test
came, were not afraid to pay the price for their convictions and beliefs.

Listen to what several of them said after they were sentenced to death:

Father Alfred Delp, a Jesuit priest from Mannheim:

"Bread is important, freedom is more important but most important of all is loyalty to your faith and steadfastness in worship."

Helmuth James Graf von Moltke, expert on international law, wrote this in a letter to his wife:

"And he (your husband) stands before Freisler not as a Protestant, not as a landowner, not as a nobleman, a Prussian or a German... but as a Christian. That and nothing else".

Julius Leber, editor and journalist:

From prison in 1933 he wrote: "One can terrorise the people by every possible means but love can grow only out of humanity and justice. And without love there is no fatherland."

Before his execution he sent his friends this message: "For so good and just a cause the sacrifice of one's life is the appropriate price."

Love Grandad

THE HOMING INSTINCT

Dear Patrick, I know how interested you are in nature and the environment so I thought you'd appreciate this story.

One of my favourite TV programmes is the series on the natural world usually presented by David Attenborough. I recall a fascinating one on bird migration which to me is one of the most wonderful and dramatic events imaginable. Here is a flock of geese or swans or ducks or swallows moving across the sky in perfect formation and harmony with each other. For some birds these migrations cover huge distances. For example the Arctic terns travel as much as thirty five thousand kilometres every year.

Besides changing weather conditions many birds seem to have an inborn 'calendar' that tells them when to migrate. Research shows that the birds use a number of ways to gather directional information during their flights. Many are guided by the sun, moon and stars. Others follow landscape features such as coastlines, rivers or mountain ranges.

Whenever I think about this marvel of nature I recall how the Danish theologian, Soren Kierkegaard described the flight of wild ducks:

'Once there was a wild duck used to the tractless wilderness of the air. On one of his migrations to the north he chanced to alight in a farm-yard where tame ducks were being fed. He ate some of their corn and liked it so much that he lingered until the next meal, then on through the next day, then the next month until autumn came and his old companions flew over the farm-yard and gave their cry to him, that it was time for him to be away. The old ecstacy roused within him again and he flapped his wings in order to join them but alas he could not leave the ground. He had grown fat on the farmer's corn and the lazy life of the farmyard. So he resigned himself to stay there, and each season until his death the calls of his fellows roused him but each year the calls came fainter and further away. The wild duck had become a tame duck'

This is a profound and challenging story, because it is a parable of what it means to be a human being, free to make choices about how we should live. It makes us ask ourselves what our values are and what are the priorities in our lives, or as we say 'what makes us tick?'

It is here that the New Testament gives us such a radical response. It does not talk about "musts" and "must nots" or rules and regulations. Above all else it centres on a person who lived among us and it describes what He said and what He did. Frequently it outlines the claims He made for himself. He explained that He and His Father were one that He was the Way, the Truth and the Life and matched what He

said by what He did. But He did not stop there He promised that he would always be with us to guide and direct us.

I will never forget one time in 1985. Granny and I had to travel through Berlin when it was still a divided city. We were in the east and wanted to return to the west. I should say that I am not very good at reading maps or following verbal instructions.

When we arrived at the station in the east, it was very crowded and very quickly we were lost and the passers by had no time to stop and we had the sense of being really isolated and forgotten. Then suddenly the unexpected happened. A large man, himself a Polish stranger and slightly inebriated, stopped and realised our problem. He paused for a moment, lifted our bags and then said in broken English, "I go with you and take you there."

That made all the difference and that is the heart of the Christian Way. Not just good advice but the unfailing promise to be with us all the way!"

Love Grandad

THE UNFINISHED JOURNEY

Dear Patrick, I am sure you, as a rugby player, will appreciate this letter. What a pity the Welsh teams don't come to Ravenhill now!

One of my most vivid memories I have as a young schoolboy is of going to watch an International Rugby match at Ravenhill Park ground in Belfast. True I do not remember the date or indeed the result. But what I do remember was the huge crowd of Welsh supporters with their red berets and scarves and of course leeks, the national emblem of their country. A large number of them were coal miners who had come from the Rhonda Valley and other mining areas.

I vividly remember the unforgettable singing of the Welsh supporters and what a fine repertoire of songs they could sing in harmony and what an enjoyable way it was to spend the long wait before the kick-off.

There was one item I will always remember and that was just before the start of the game. Indeed I am sure the Welsh considered it as their special piece and who could blame them. It was a very rousing Welsh tune and it gave great confidence and inspiration to their team, as they stood to sing it with the greatest fervour and pride. It was a living affirmation of their country, people and team.

'Guide me, O Thou great Jehovah,
Pilgrim through this barren land;
I am weak, but thou art mighty,
Hold me with thy powerful hand;
Bread of heaven, Bread of heaven
Feed me till my want is o'er.'

But was the fervour and passion with which these words were sung just a 'battle song' to bolster the morale of their team before the contest started? It is at least worth considering. The theme of the hymn is about the journey we are all making. And everyone of us immediately identifies with it. It is this same theme that runs right through all the literature of the ages. Think of the vast number of stories that have been written through the centuries. The most common and lasting themes have been those about pilgrimages, odysseys, voyages, and explorations. Remember stories such as the Iliad of Homer, the Pilgrim's Progress, the Canterbury Tales, and indeed the theme of the Bible.

I can think of the very different times and places when I remember singing this hymn and the amazing manner in which it seems to fit into so many very different situations. It was the most popular hymn sung on our troopship in 1940 when we had to circumnavigate Africa to get to Egypt in a convoy of ten liners and face the daily menace of air attack from above and submarine torpedoes from below. Or again how often it was sung in the squalor and hunger of a prisoner-of-war camp. Then how it came up again as peace and freedom were celebrated. It is in fact a hymn for all seasons!It deals with our everyday lives and experiences.

Whether we would describe ourselves as religious or not, we understand that indeed we are on the move and that time marches on. Our watches and calendars, as well as the changes in our bodies, remind us that our lives are never static but dynamic. As we grasp that, we cannot but ask where it leads to,how will it all end? Is it just an accident? Will it be an unending cycle? Will we simply fade away? Is it a cul-de-sac,a round-about? Or will it be the great highway to a richer and fuller life? Right through the years of my journey, with all its ups and downs, I go back again and again to these lines written by the American poet J.G. Whittier:

I know not what the future holds
Of marvel or surprise
Assured by this, that life and death
His mercy underlies.

I know not where His islands lift
Their fronded palms in air
I only know I cannot drift
Beyond his love and care.

To me that says it all.

Love Grandad

WHAT IS PRAYER?

Dear Patrick, I'm sure you have seen the film 'Titanic'. I found it one of the most moving I have ever seen.

Of course it has very special interest for Belfast, as its tragic story is very much part of our history, although it dates back to 1912. This film has already broken all records and proves to be an unforgettable experience for all who have seen it. The impact is not merely due to the power of modern technology but to a large extent to the sense that this is a real event and actually took place. There were many unforget-table scenes and I think of one of the most powerful towards the end, when everybody realised that the ship was doomed, as it began gently tilting and then to sink. Many distraught passengers gathered round a minister of religion who leads them in prayer. I imagine many of them had not prayed for a very long time, but now as the end draws near, they all pray as never before.

Of course this was a very understandable response at such a time, but it is very sad when people choose to limit prayer to such extreme situations and only look on it as a last resort. They forget that it embraces the whole of life and human experience and cannot be confined to such unusual and extreme circumstances.

Let us talk about faith in its simplest and basic sense. We ask what the core of it is. It is above all else about relationship and if this is to be real there must be communication between God and man. Indeed all the great religions affirm this. We have to emphasise this, however, because even practising church members have not grasped this truth and think that the essence of their religion is to keep the moral code. Indeed this is part of the Christian life, but on its own it is a very colourless and legalistic way to live and has little to do with the real thing.

If a relationship between two people is to be real and living, there has to be communication. I can think about it in terms of my own relationship with Granny. I had known her as a fellow student in Queen's University and - how shall I put it? - I was 'interested' in her. But that was all. Then the war came and I had to make a long voyage to Egypt in convoy. It took seven weeks, as we had to circumnavigate Africa, as the Italians blocked the direct route through the Mediterranean. As the weeks passed I began to think about Granny. I debated whether I should write or not. I realised that if I did not write, there could be no real relationship. So one day on the long trip around Africa, I did write and that letter was the first step in what has turned out to be a life-long relationship. Yes, relationships do depend on communication.

Communication is the life line of all our relationships and this is why prayer is so important and so central in the lives of the multitudes of men and women through the ages and in the life of Christ himself. I am sure that without it we are like fish without water or a sailor without the sea. I would go on to say that it is the driving force of faith. But in a living relationship we don't communicate just when we want something. or like the passengers on the Titanic when we are in an extreme situation. Real relationships mean so much more than that. It means that we are willing not just to share the unimportant and trivial things in life but the significant and real issues. Perhaps you have had the experience of talking to someone at superficial level. Then something is said that sparks a very real and living dialogue and exchange and somehow you begin to see that person in a new light. There is a real meeting of minds and a new mutual understanding happens. We get to know the other person. When that begins to happen you become open to each another. You are no longer afraid to talk of your failures and weaknesses and are free to discuss the good and happy experiences of life and acknowledge how much you have to be grateful for and are secure enough to share your problems and fears and ask for support and understanding. A relationship like this helps us to understand what prayer is meant to be and it was in this way that Jesus related to the disciples and does still to his followers of all ages and times.

Such a relationship and such prayer is not to be confined to set formal occasions - important as they are. I like to think of prayer as a continuous dialogue or conversation that goes on all the time and right through our lives.

'Religious experience' as Archbishop Temple said 'is the whole experience of the religious man'. Whenever I think back over my own life right from the earliest days I can remember that unending dialogue I had with Christ. It would be about my life at school - relationships, examinations, sport and all the problems and challenges that a school boy has to face. It was a similar pattern at the university; then life in the desert; followed by various prison camps in Italy and Germany. The importance and reality of that continuing dialogue has stayed with me all my life and it is at the heart of my religious belief. I go over and over again those promises of Christ to his followers: 'I am with you always', You are my friends','Abide in me as I abide in you' and they have made all the difference!

Love Grandad

A DIFFERENT M.O.T.TEST

Dear Patrick, I believe you have got your driving licence recently so you will be familiar with M.O.T. requirements.

As I look at the tax disc on my car I am reminded that another M.O.T is rapidly approaching. Initially I have mixed feelings when, on the one hand, I think of making an appointment on a certain date, queuing up with a line of other cars at the testing yard, checking the brakes, lights,gears, clutch etc etc. But on the other hand I am relieved to be assured by the experts that my car is in perfect condition and is unlikely to let me down.

As I thought about that annual event and its importance, I came to the conclusion that if motor cars need such a regular test, if they are to perform properly, so do human beings. From time to time we need a personal M.O.T. It is very easy in the wear and tear of everyday life for us to become careless and thoughtless,drifting into set attitudes and practices, without thinking about what is happening to us or let others decide for us. When we do that we are really surrendering our freedom and our humaness. The essence of being a real person is to use the gift of our freedom to make our own choices and decide how we live our lives and use our gifts and opportunities.

It is vital from time to time that we sit down and ask ourselves the real questions. What are the really important things in my life? Are they power, influence, prestige? Am I self centred? Do I really care about other people? Write out a really honest statement of what you want most in life and how you see yourself today. Consider the changes you would like to make in your lifestyle.

I would suggest that a very appropriate moral and spiritual M.O.T is the Prayer of St Francis. Incidentally these words are inscribed on the glass door at the entrance to the Croi at Corrymeela.

Lord, make me an instrument of your peace
Where there is hatred, let me sow love
Where there is injury, pardon
Where there is doubt, faith
Where their is despair, hope
Where there is darkness, light
Where there is sadness, joy
O Divine Master, grant that I might not so much seek to be
Consoled as to console
To be understood as to understand
To be loved as to love

For it is in giving that we receive
It is in pardoning that we are pardoned
It is in dying that we are born to eternal life.

Love Grandad

AND JESUS WEPT

Dear Patrick, No doubt you have seen on TV some of the tragic events in the Omagh inquiry. This is an article I wrote shortly after the bombing.

Omagh, Co.Tyrone. 3.10 PM, 15th August 1998.

A day that will be forever remembered in Ireland, a day when 29 men, women and children were suddenly and horribly killed and others seriously injured.

The bomb had been detonated in the heart of a busy provincial town at the peak of shopping time, when the streets were crowded: mothers with their children buying blazers, shirts and shoes for the new term at school; young people with holiday jobs in the shops to earn some pocket money; older people having a look round and meeting up with their friends for a chat; shop keepers and their assistants very busy with so many likely customers. Just an ordinary Saturday afternoon in a bustling country town.

Then at 3.10pm life was suddenly shattered and transformed for multitudes of people - never to be the same again.

A terrorist bomb had exploded right in the heart of the town. Indescribable scenes followed, too harrowing to try to describe; bodies were blown to pieces, limbs scattered in the street, blood streaming everywhere; events that rendered even the most experienced media people struggling to control their feelings and find words to describe what they saw.

Still, six days later, one's thoughts were kept rivetted to this town; the people, the hospital, the broken-hearted mums and dads, husbands and wives, brothers and sisters. Then the slow realisation that this was just the start of a long journey of grief and irrepressible loss and the knowledge for so many that life would never be the same again. It seemed to be an unending six days with so many funerals, the agonising processions, the church services, the tributes and prayers and, indeed, the body language that at times expressed the unspeakable.

Several questions keep surfacing in the mind: Will this terrible, obscene massacre of innocent people going about their everyday lives be at last the catalyst that will bring everyone to their senses? Will it create an overwhelming determination from all in our community that such a barbaric event can never take place again? Is this a definitive event in our history, as we are confronted by the terrible logic of a ruthless, mindless violence and its unspeakable results? It is not an ultimatum that compels us to reassess all our political and human values? This is an event that takes us to the brink and cries out to us that we must give all we have and are to find a new way together.

Another thought that came to me, as I watched those moving, heart rendering interviews with some of the relatives, is of the value of life to each one of us: the gift of our families, our friends and relationships; of the utter importance of cherishing them and not taking them for granted. Indeed, just the knowledge that we love and are loved and that nothing can destroy that.

There is one other thought and it must be in the minds of many people, as we try to come to terms with what has happened at Omagh. It is just the simple question - where then is God in all of this? Why did He allow it to happen? There is no slick or easy answer.

Indeed, to find one we have to go right to the heart of the Gospel. As Christians we believe in a God of love. This is the central message of the Bible.

What happened at Omagh breaks the heart of God. Indeed, as He is infinite love He is hurt as we are - only infinitely more. Why then did He allow it to happen? Why then, we may respond, did he allow the Cross to happen? Because we are free to choose how we live and what we do for our own interests and our cause and none of us can claim to be innocent. God does not force or compel; that is never His way of love. On the contrary, He enters into our suffering and pain. Jesus wept over Jerusalem, as he saw the terrible results of the blindness, prejudice and hate of its inhabitants, and the Cross showed how he cared.

These lines of Studdert Kennedy, written from the horror and bloodshed of the trenches in World War 1, seem to express something of what I am trying to say:

How can it be that God can reign in glory,
Calmly content with what His love has done,
Reading unmoved the piteous shameful story,
And the vile deeds men do beneath the sun?

Are there no tears in the Eternal?
Is there no pain to pierce the soul of God?
Then must He be a fiend of Hell infernal,
Beating the earth to pieces with His rod.

Father, if he, the Christ, was Thy Revealer
Truly the first begotten of the Lord
Then must Thou be a Sufferer and a Healer,
Pierced to the heart by the sorrow of the sword.
Then must it mean, not only that Thy sorrow
Smote thee that once upon the lonely tree,

But that today, tonight, and on the morrow,
Still will it come O Gallant God, to Thee.

Love Grandad

DEPARTMENTALISM

Dear Patrick, I believe this is a very important question for each of us. Can we really live our lives in separate compartments?

President Clinton's relationship with Monica Lewinsky, one of the White House staff, has sparked off once again the perennial debate - should a politician's political life stand apart from his behaviour in private life? This has been debated for many months all over the world and has certainly dominated the last period of Bill Clinton's Presidency.

But it does raise a very important issue for us all, as we think about how we live our lives. There is a very wide belief that our religious faith and practice can be isolated and become a detached part of our lives. Lord Melbourne, a Prime Minister in the Victorian era, gives classic expression of this practice when he remarked; "Things have come to a pretty pass, if religion was going to interfere with affairs of private life"

This approach seems to me to lead to a great misunderstanding of the Christian Faith. It seems to reduce it to a habit, an activity, an interest, indeed a hobby. It reminds me of the old jingle:

It's what they do on Sunday
They'll be alright on Monday
It's a little habit they have all acquired.

More seriously it seems to suggest that God is only interested and involved in a part of our lives and that being a believer is only a part time activity. It puts it on the same level as joining a painting class or keep fit club.

But this is surely a tragic interpretation of the Faith and indeed of God Himself.

The earliest description of what Christianity was was "The Way". Indeed this was the word that was used from the beginning to describe the life of a follower of Christ. It is not just what we believe but how we live. It is a way of living the whole of life; our thinking and doing. It is not just about debating, discussing and reading the latest books on theology, but how we incarnate and express this knowledge. Think of the words of the Great Commandment: 'Love the Lord your God with all your heart, all your soul and all your mind' and 'Love your neighbour as you love yourself'. There is no suggestion of a part time or a departmental commitment. We believe in a God who cares infinitely about the whole of our lives and all our activities. This is how William Temple explains it, 'Religious experience is the whole experience of the religious man'. And again: 'It is a great mistake to suppose that God is interested only, or primarily in religion'

I like what Paul Tournier, a Swiss doctor and counsellor, said "For the fulfilment of his purpose God needs more than priests, bishops, pastors and missionaries. He needs mechanics and chemists, gardeners and street cleaners, dressmakers and cooks, physicians, philosophers, judges and short hand typist's. The tragedy is that so many people have a small picture of God and think of him in a very narrow way, forgetting that 'He is the Lord and Creator of the whole universe. I sometimes like to watch the Television programme "Tomorrow's World" or David Attenborough's ecology films. They remind me of the endless variety, beauty, dynamic and incredibility of this world we live in. Think of some of the Psalms, like the majestic 19th:

"The heavens declare the glory of God and the earth shows forth his handiwork". Or Psalm 8: "When I consider the heavens, the work of your fingers, the moon and the stars, which you have ordained; what is man that you are mindful of him or the son of man, that you visit him?"

Of course the life and worship of the Church is vital. But it must never be seen as an end in itself. Rather its purpose is to focus us and our energy on all of life, on the world that God loves. I like to think of the Church as a service station, where we are equipped for our tasks in the world wherever they may be: the kitchen, the office, the school, the factory or the desk.

These words by George McLeod, founder of the Iona Community, put it in a nutshell: "The departmentalising of religion is appalling. It used to be the Queen of the sciences with other forms of knowledge, like attendant courtiers working out the ordering of the Queen and doing her bidding. Religion is now the Cinderella of the sciences some-where in the basement... The two ugly sisters of economics and politics now control the sciences... This is appalling, because the very genius of the Hebrew tradition is its relatedness". In the words of John MacMurray "The great contribution of the Hebrews to religion was that they did away with it". All previous religions had been concerned with the soul and its journey through a negative religious order. The Hebrew faith was the first to be concerned with the whole, with the redemption of the material, with the recreation of the whole person".

Love Grandad

GRAFFITI

Dear Patrick, When you come to Belfast to visit us you cannot but see the numerous and elaborate wall-paintings or graffiti

Whether we like them or not they are very much a part of our everyday lives especially if we live in a city or large town. Some are just crude drawings or written obscenities, clever slogans, names and trademarks of particular groups or gangs or just the simple desire of self expression. They suggest a variety of motives: amusement, propaganda, information or just frustration.

This method of communication is as old as civilization itself. It is found in the ancient monuments of Egypt. Indeed these are greatly valued by linguists and historians, as they take us much closer to the spoken language of that period and help us to understand what ordinary life was like in the ancient world.

They are a very real and inescapable part of our lives here in Northern Ireland and a very chastening warning of how divided our country is in so many different ways: political, religious, historical and social.

One of the oldest and best known examples of graffiti is to be found in Rome. It is a very vivid and potent reminder that being a Christian has often been a very costly and life threatening affair. Many untrue stories were circulated about the Christians which made the hatred of the pagans all the greater. For example the Emperor Nero charged the Christians with setting fire to Rome. He really did it himself, but shifted the blame to the Christians and had many of them nailed to crosses and covered with tar and burned in his garden as torches, by night.

This rough drawing is an example of graffiti from this time. It helps us to understand something of the current attitude against Christians and the silly rumours that were circulating about the followers of Christ in Rome. The crowds began to pass round the story that Christians worshipped a donkey's head. Someone scratched this story on a wall. The Greek words mean - "Alexamenos worships his God"

Many other charges were brought against the Christians. They were said to be cannibals and eat babies. This story started because the Lord's Supper was practiced in secret. The people did not know what happened at these secret meetings but they heard that someone was being eaten. Jesus had said at the Last Supper, "This bread is my body, this wine my blood". The people who heard this assumed that the Christians were eating and drinking human flesh and blood. The mob thought that people who did such terrible deeds, if allowed to live, would bring all sorts of trouble on the land. Such wickedness would stir

up the gods who would punish not only the Christians, but those who allowed them to exist. So when the cattle died or the river Tiber overflowed its banks, the people said 'See! Let us throw the Christians to the lions'.

The story of Polycarp, the aged bishop of Smyrna around 150 AD brings home to us how terrifying and cruel those times were. He was imprisoned, because he refused to betray his Christian belief by declaring 'Caesar is Lord' and putting incense on his altar. When he refused he was brought to the Colloseum to be thrown to the lions. But the prison governor gave him three chances to save his life. First he was ordered to say, 'Away with the Atheists!' Polycarp pointed to the heathen in the galleries and said 'Away with the Atheists!' He was given another chance, 'Curse Christ'. He answered, "Eight and sixty years have I served him and he has done me no wrong, and can I revile my King that saved me?" A third time the governor said, 'Swear by Caesar'. Polycarp replied, 'I am a Christian. If you want to know what that is, set a day and listen'. Finally as Polycarp refused to swear by Caesar, the governor made his final threat: "If you refuse I'll throw you to the beasts". "Bring on your beasts", said Polycarp "Then if you scorn the beasts I'll have you burned." said the governor. Finally he was burned at the stake. As I remember those first martyrs and the price they paid to preserve the faith for those who came after, I ask myself how much does my faith cost me and how far would I go to preserve and pass it on?

All through my life I have gone back time and time again to that wonderful chapter in the 11th chapter of Hebrews. The writer paints an unforgettable picture of that succession of men and women who through the ages have endured incredible hardship and suffering to pass on their faith to us today. Then it comes to a wonderful climax in the opening verse of the next chapter. I am sure the writer must have attended the Olympic Games and seen the great collection of athletes striving to win through. The writer sees this as an image of the great race in which we are all involved. I like to think of it as a relay race in which we receive the baton from those who have gone before us and pass it on to those who follow after us.

"Surrounded as we are by these serried ranks of witnesses, let us strip off everything that hinders us, as well as the sin which dogs our feet, and let us run the race we have to run with patience, our eyes fixed on Jesus, the source and goal of our faith"

Love Grandad

IN TOUCH WITH GREATNESS

Dear Patrick, I am sure you will have visited Chartwell as you live so near at hand.

A few months ago I was in London and had the opportunity of visiting Chartwell, the home of Winston Churchill. To me it was a fascinating experience because it brought back very vivid memories of the war-time years, as somehow Churchill seemed to epitomise that unforgettable time. In those early months of the war the whole of life and indeed civilisation seemed to be in the balance. I will never forget the anxiety and uncertainty of the late thirties and early forties: the Battle of France, the Dunkirk epic, the occupation of France, the blitz on London, the invasion threat and the Battle of Britain.

All these memories crowded back, as we were conducted round the great house of Chartwell. Here Churchill had entertained many of the famous political and military leaders of the time. Here he must have spent hours and hours of anguish and uncertainty, as one grim event followed another in the early part of the war, as he followed the ever changing maps of the Western Front, later the Middle East, the Eastern Front, and the Far East. But it was here also that he penned those unforgettable speeches that inspired new hope in the hearts of those who heard them. Indeed Job's words of long ago relived again: "Your words kept men on their feet." No one who heard them will ever forget the strength and inspiration they brought.This was part of a speech he made in the House of commons in 1940: "We shall not flag or fail. We shall go on until the end... We shall fight in the seas and oceans... We shall defend our island no matter what the cost may be,"

Then in a speech to the British people also in 1940 he said: "Let us therefore brace ourselves to our duties, and so bear ourselves that, if the British Empire and its commonwealth should last for a thousand years, men still will say, 'this was their finest hour'."

There are indeed many kinds of greatness to consider. We think of the acclaim given to film stars, TV personalities and sports champions. Those who feature in the popular TV programme - "This is Your Life" illustrate the great variety of greatness that is recognised. As we watch such programmes we may ask ourselves what is true greatness. Is it to do with talent, achievement, fortune, personality or character?

Probably if asked about greatness, multitudes would put Jesus Christ at the top of the pole. For 2000 years after his crucifixion more than 950 million people follow him. Even so we have to ask ourselves and others how far have we followed him? How closely have we looked at his life-style? How intently have we listened to some of the things he said and really understood their meaning?

I am sure that we all have to keep on learning what Christ meant whenever he spoke about greatness. It had little to do with wealth or cleverness or power or influence. In fact it is very chastening and even upsetting to think of some of the things he said about greatness, because they turn the conventional and contemporary ideas upside down. The trouble is that we are adept at reading the comfortable reassuring passages in the Bible and glossing over the hard challenging bits. Rather like the way we used to hope our parents would read our school reports. Indeed to the end, Christ's disciples could not give up their selfish ideas of greatness. In fact at the Last Supper they had a row among themselves, as to who was to be regarded as the greatest. Jesus rejects the current idea of greatness and rebukes them - "Let the greatest among you become as the youngest and the leader as the one who serves... I am among you as one who serves."

Jesus didn't just talk about this greatness, he lived it out. He was indeed supremely "the man for others". Think of that incident in the Upper Room on the eve of his crucifixion and how he longed for his disciples to get his message of loving, giving and serving others. And how terribly slow they were to grasp the point. Then he rolls up his sleeves, takes a basin of water and a towel and washes their feet, one of the humblest and most caring things that one person can do for another. This was his way of showing them that true greatness was in serving and giving.

In our broken society it is heartening to identify that great number of people who do in their life style follow Christ's call to give, serve and care for others. The examples that come readily to me are those who come from all over these islands and far beyond to serve in the Corrymeela Summer Programme. Most of them give up their holidays to come to Ballycastle. The idea of this programme is to provide holidays for those who cannot afford them. These helpers come to work in the kitchen, to care for young children, to help with the programme, to look after handicapped, to man the tuck shop, drive busses, organise trips to the beach and barbecues. These people from all over the world and of every age, are the very life blood of Corrymeela.

Love Grandad

WHAT'S THE BIG IDEA ANYWAY?

Dear Patrick, I know you've just got back from your rugby tour in America and I thought this quote might appeal to you.

This question is part of a quotation from an American writer called Clarence Darrow. He prefixes the question with these words, "We are born, we stick around for a while, we die. What's the big idea anyway?" That is a question that most of us ask sooner or later in the course of our lives. When I was a student at the university and occasionally attended student functions like club or society dinners, the introduction that every would-be speaker had to endure as he or she rose to their feet was the intimidating choral ditty:

Why were you born so beautiful
Why were you born at all ?
You're no b... use for anything
You're no b... use at all.

Even so it is a very basic question and what follows is a plain man's attempt to pursue it. If I may change the tone a little I will quote the Apostle Peter's advice in his first letter:

'Always have your answer ready for people who ask you the reason for the hope you all have'.

I have therefore decided to respond to this question because I believe it is the most important one that can be asked. It is indeed the ultimate question. In other words it involves all of me not just my intellect. It involves the total me - intellectually, emotionally, morally and spiritually. Existential philosophers would say that I answer this question with my whole life at stake. It is, for example, the action a person must take, if he is walking up a very steep and narrow road and suddenly he sees a massive steam tractor hurtling down the hill towards him and seemingly out of control. He has to decide instantly what to do, because his whole life is at imminent risk. Do you remember how Jesus answered when he was asked which was the greatest command-ment? "You shall love the Lord your God with all your heart, and with all your soul, and with all your mind and with all your strength." It is to be total - all of me and of you.

There are two sorts of questions that life throws at us. There are the HOW questions and the WHY questions. Today our society is expert at answering the HOW questions.

I am simply amazed when I think of the scientific and technological revolution that is taking place. I am amazed by what my grandchildren can do with their computers and the vast range of knowledge that is now available at our fingertips. I consider the huge acceleration of invention and knowledge that has taken place in my life time. Think of the space shots, landing on the Moon, and tele-communication. The KNOW HOW is accumulating all the time. But we know only too well that it is not all a cause for celebration. There are many shadows across our screens. True that we may have learned to sail across the seas, to fly around the world, to rocket to the moon, but we have yet to learn how to walk the earth in peace.

So then it is not enough to know HOW to do things we have also to face the question WHY? What's the big idea anyway?" I am a follower of Christ because he helps me to deal with the WHY questions, the really ultimate ones that we don't talk about very often, but that are in the back of everyone's mind. Such questions as "Why am I here?" "What is life really about?" "What should I do with my life?" "Can I live just for myself?" "How do I know what choices I should make?" "What about the future when this life is over?"

So I write because I believe the Way of Christ makes sense out of life not only for me but for others. I believe because this Faith really helps me to understand who I am, what I am here for and how I should live. It helps me to face the future in this life and what is to come in the next. All these things are what the Big Idea is all about.

This was how it was put by a famous Army Chaplain of the First World War, Studdert Kennedy or 'Woodbine Willie', as he was known by the soldiers in the trenches:

> How do I know that God is good? I don't.
> I gamble like a man. I bet my life upon one side in life's great war. I must.
> I can't stand out. I must take sides.
> The man who is neutral in this fight is not
> A man. He's bulk and body without breath.
> I want to live, live out, not wobble through my life somehow, and then into the dark.
> I must have God. This life's too dull without.

Love Grandad

THE RABBI'S GIFT

Dear Peter, This is quite a subtle story and worth thinking about. It is told by Dr Scott Peck, the American writer, in his book "The Different Drum".

The story concerns a monastery that had fallen upon hard times. Once a great order, as a result of waves of anti-monastic persecution in the 17th and 18th centuries and the rise of secularism in the 19th, all its branch houses were lost and and it had become decimated to the extent that there were only five monks left in the decaying mother house: the abbot and four others, all over seventy in age. Clearly it was a dying order.

In the deep woods surrounding the monastery there was a little hut that a rabbi from a nearby town occasionally used for a hermitage. Through their many years of prayer and contemplation the old monks had become a bit psychic, so they could always sense when the rabbi was in his hermitage. "The rabbi is in the woods, the rabbi is in the woods again," they would whisper to each other. As he agonised over the imminent death of his order, it occurred to the abbot at one such time to visit the hermitage and ask the rabbi, if by any chance, he could offer any advice that might save the monastery.

The rabbi welcomed the abbot at his hut. But when the abbot explained the purpose of his visit, the rabbi could only commiserate with him. "I know how it is," he exclaimed, The spirit has gone out of the people. It is the same in my town. Almost no one comes to the synagogue any more." So the old abbot and the old rabbi wept together. Then they read parts of the Torah and quietly spoke of deep things. The time came when the abbot had to leave. They embraced each other. "It has been a wonderful thing that we should meet after all these years," the abbot said, "but I have still failed in my purpose for coming here. Is there nothing you can tell me, no piece of advice you can give me that would help me save my dying order?"

"No, I am sorry," the rabbi responded. "I have no advice to give. The only thing I can tell you is that the Messiah is one of you."

In the days and weeks and months that followed, the old monks pondered this and wondered whether there was any possible significance to the rabbi's words. The Messiah is one of us? Could he possibly have meant one of us monks here at the monastery? If that's the case, which one? Do you suppose he meant the abbot? Yes, if he meant anyone, he probably meant Father Abbott. He has been our leader for more than a generation. On the other hand, he might have meant Brother Thomas. Certainly Thomas was a man of light. Certainly he could not have meant Brother Elred! Elred gets crotchety at times. But come to think of it, even though he is a thorn in people's sides, when you look back on it, Elred is virtually always right.Often very right. Maybe the rabbi did mean brother Elred. But surely not Brother Phillip. Phillip is so passive, a real nobody. But then, almost myster-iously, he has a gift somehow of always being there when you need him. He just magically appears by your side. Maybe Phillip is the Messiah. Of course the rabbi didn't mean me. He couldn't possibly have meant me. I'm just an ordinary person. Yet supposing he did? Suppose I am the Messiah? O, God, not me. I couldn't be that much for You, could I?

As they contemplated in this manner, the old monks began to treat each other with extraordinary respect on the off chance that one among them might be the Messiah. And on the off, off chance that each monk himself might be the Messiah, they began to treat themselves with extraordinary respect.

Because the forest in which it was situated was beautiful, it so happened that people still occasionally came to visit the monastery to picnic on its tiny lawn, to wander along some of its paths, even now and then to go into the dilapidated chapel to meditate. As they did so, without even being conscious of it, they sensed this aura of extra-ordinary respect that now began to surround the five old monks and seemed to radiate out from them and permeate the atmosphere of the place. There was something strangely attractive, even compelling, about it. Hardly knowing why, they began to come back to the monastery more frequently to picnic, to play, to pray. They began to bring their friends to show them this special place. And their friends brought their friends.

Then it happened that some of the younger men came to visit the monastery started to talk more and more with the old monks. After a while one asked if he could join them. Then another. And another. So within a few years the monastery had once again become a thriving order and, thanks to the rabbi's gift, a vibrant centre of light and spirituality in the realm.

Love Grandad

ENJOYING RELIGION

Dear Peter, Here is a about Africa which I am sure you will enjoy.

It is the story told of a missionary in a dark corner of Africa where the men had the habit of filing away their teeth to sharp points. He was hard at work trying to convert a native chief. Now the chief was very old and the missionary was very Old Testament. His version of Christianity leaned heavily on the thou-shalt-nots. The savage listened patiently.

"I don't understand," he said at last. "You tell me that I should not take my neighbour's wife."

"That's right," said the missionary.

"Or his ivory or his oxen."

"Quite right."

"And I must not dance the war dance and then ambush him on the trail and kill him."

"Absolutely right."

"But I cannot do any of these things," said the savage regretfully. "I am too old. To be old is to be a Christian. They are the same thing."

Alas, that is the image that many young people have of Christianity. It is something old, joyless, insipid and negative. It is putting a brake on real life. That is how many of us both inside the church and out have reduced the Good-News out of Nazareth to a list of thou-shalt-nots. The result is that multitudes of lively young adults have been turned off and led to feel that the Christian Faith is not their thing. And there are those who like to encourage this idea, as it fits in with their desire to exploit youth for their own gain.

Of course we Christians have humbly to acknowledge that we have helped to create this negative impression that the Faith is stuffy, old hat and not geared for today. It is all too true that "some have been so heavenly minded that they are of no earthly use." But if you really look at the evidence, you'll get another very different picture. The church has existed for 2000 years and today there are 950 million Christians in the world. It has passed through many vicissitudes. It has had its dark ages. But the amazing thing is that it has refused to die. It has survived. Why has this been so? Because at its heart there has always been the deathless message of Life, Hope and Joy. Because the church has always believed in Resurrection and the amazing belief that Jesus is alive.

What lies behind that incredible belief? Surely above all else the need to grasp and take in the fact that God is love: that is his reason for creating us and our world. We must know this, if we are to get the message. But in this world that he has created in love, there is much that resists and wants to destroy love. We know all too well, when we are honest with ourselves, that we too are part of the greed, pride, rivalry and indeed hate that destroys life. How then does this God of infinite love handle it?

God in Jesus Christ confronts evil. He takes it at its worst in the hatred, greed, deceit and cowardice that combined to cause his Crucifixion at Calvary. In this, human selfishness and enmity did their utmost to destroy him and his kingdom of love. But they failed to break his spirit and at the climax he was able to pray in his dying agony, "Father, forgive them for they know not what they do." Then there was the Resurrection, the empty tomb and Christ risen and alive for always.

Try to understand the wonder, amazement and joy of those who were there. They gradually came to terms with what it meant. All the hopes they had for him were true. All his promises were being fulfilled. Something that was cosmic in its meaning had happened here at the empty tomb. That the most terrible deed that man could do to Christ was transformed into an overwhelming victory over all evil, pride, greed, hate and death itself. No wonder that the great recurring call to the followers of Christ is "Rejoice in the Lord always."

In the early 1920s in Russia, one of the Communist leaders, Bucharin, was sent from Moscow to Kiev to address a vast anti-God rally. For one hour he brought to bear all the artillery of argument, abuse and ridicule upon the Christian faith until it seemed as if the whole structure of belief was in ruins. At the end there was silence. Questions were invited. A man rose and asked leave to speak. He was a priest of the Orthodox Church. He stood beside Bucharin, faced the people and gave them the ancient Easter greeting, "CHRIST IS RISEN." In an instant the whole assembly rose to its feet and the reply came back like the crash of breakers against a cliff, "HE IS RISEN INDEED!" There was no reply, there could not be.

Love Grandad

FIERCE FEATHERS

Dear Peter, I know you have been to America, but I wonder if you have ever heard this story?

It happened in the summer of the year 1775, away out in America, in Easton near New York.

The children had come with their parents to the little Church or Meeting House, as they called it, right out in the country. It was a very unusual Church unlike any you have ever seen in this country. It was made of logs that did not fit quite close together and if a boy or girl happened to be sitting in the corner, through a chink they could see right out into the woods. For the Meeting House was surrounded by the untamed wilderness that stretched away on all sides around the newly cleared settlement of Easton.

They were Quakers or Friends, as they like to be called. Everybody seemed to find it hard to worship today and even the face of Zebulon Hoxie, the grandfather of most of the children, wore traces of anxiety.

The children had never before seen one of the stranger Friends who sat in the gallery by their grandfather's side. For Robert Nisbet had just arrived, after having walked for two days, to meet with the Friends at their mid-week meeting.

The children did not know why he had come but they liked his kind open face and were glad when he rose to speak. But they liked the words of his text even better. "The beloved of the Lord shall dwell in safety by him. He shall cover them all the day long with his feathers..." After he had said this he lingered for a moment and then gravely he continued. "You have done well, dear friends, to stay on valiantly in your homes, when all your neighbours have fled. These promises of covering and shelter are truly meant for you. Make them your own and you shall not be afraid for the terror by night nor the arrow that flieth by day."

Dinah, Mrs Hoxie's youngest daughter began to think of feathers, thinking of the words of the speaker, "He shall cover them with his feathers and under His wings shalt thou trust." Just as she was thinking she turned her head towards the wall and there through the chink she could see - feathers: red, yellow, blue and pink. What could they be? Then suddenly they were gone.

Mrs Hoxie looked through the slit in the wall as her little daughter had done and there saw the same feathers. Then she saw three feathers creeping above the sill of the open meeting house window. For just one moment her heart seemed to stand still. She went white to the lips. Then the words flashed back to her... "shall dwell in safety by Him."

Her husband looked up too and there he also saw the feathers -

three, five, seven sticking up in a row. A second later and a dark-skinned face, an evil face appeared above the sill. The moment most to be dreaded in the lives of all American settlers had come to the little company in their meeting. An Indian chief was staring in at their Meeting House window, showing his teeth in a cruel grin. In his hand he held a sheaf of arrows, poisoned arrows, only too ready to fly and kill by day.

In an instant he was in through the door and all had seen him - a naked brown figure in full war paint and feathers, looking with piercing eyes at each man Friend, as if one of them must have the weapons he sought. But the Friends were entirely unarmed.

A minute later a dozen other Redskins stood beside the Chief and then they saw thirteen sharp arrows taken from their quivers and placed on the bows which were stiffened and ready to shoot. Yet, still the friends sat on without moving in complete silence.

Dinah turned and watched her grandfather and saw him gazing full at the chief. The Indian's flashing eyes under the matted black eye-brows, gazed back fiercely beneath his narrow red forehead into the Quaker's calm blue eyes beneath the white brow and snowy hair. No word was spoken but in silence two powers were matched against each other: the power of hate and the power of love. For steady friendliness to his strange visitors was written in every line of Zebulon Hoxie's face.

The children never knew how long that steadfast gaze lasted. But at last for some unknown reason the Indian's gaze fell. His head that he had carried so high and haughtily sank towards his breast. He glanced round the Meeting House with a glance that nothing could escape, then, signing to his followers, the 13 arrows were noiselessly replaced in 13 quivers and 13 bows were laid down and rested against the wall. Many footsteps, lighter that falling snow, crossed the floor. The Indian Chief unarmed, sat down himself in the nearest seat with his followers in all their warpaint, but also unarmed, close round him

The meeting did not stop - it increased in solemnity and power. Never while they lived did any of those present that day forget that silent meeting or the brooding Presence, that closer, clearer than sunlight, filled the bright room.

"He shall cover them with his feathers all the day long"

Love Grandad

LEARNING THE BASICS

Dear Peter, I wonder if like me you are keen on sport and frequently watch football, hockey or cricket on T.V.

Whether you are a spectator or performer you will realise how important it is for players to master the special skills in whatever game they play. You know that you can't expect just to start playing without any preparation or training. Every player has to spend time practising how to kick, tackle, pass, catch, field and many other things, if the game is to get enjoyable. But acquiring these skills takes time and patience. I know this from my experience of trying to play golf. I did everything wrong - the swing, the position of my legs and body and of course not keeping my eye on the ball. It was all a bit of a shambles.

If you watch sports on Television and listen to the skilled commentators describing the game and how individual players are performing, you will hear one of them say after a specially good piece of play by one of the teams: "Those forwards know all the basics." We know that to be true not only in sport but in every part of our lives. We need to be well trained and practiced in the fundamentals. Achieving anything really worthwhile in life takes time and concentration and cost. Ask a musician or an artist or a mechanic or a plumber. In all cases there are certain skills that are essential.

That opens us up to a wider question - "What are the basic skills in living?" What are the qualities that really count?" Current culture offers many answers along the lines of influence, wealth, and power. But are these adequate and do they really satisfy our whole self?

A vast number of young people today have their role models: those they admire and try to copy. Imitation is a very powerful force in our lives. We all copy others perhaps at times unconsciously. This urge to copy and imitate those people we admire is something we all do. We all have our special icon people - our role models. Such figures have a massive influence in our everyday lives. Think of the queues that line up to take part in Pop concerts and the acclaim given to the performers of the fan clubs attached to every football team. Imitation is very much part of our lives and has played a crucial part in the development of our civilisation. Of course it has varied and at times it has been a very constructive and creative force and at others negative and destructive. A brief survey of this century presents many examples of both.

One of the problems about contemporary role models is that they don't last very long. Young people's ideas change, as life moves on. The role models and icons usually have a short life and sooner or later are replaced by new ones.

Nonetheless we do need a role model, someone who will never go out of date, someone who will inspire us to be our true selves, the person we really want to be, someone who will help us to realise the inner hopes and longings that are deep down in each of us. I am sure this is what St Augustine had in mind when he said: "You have made us for yourself and our hearts are restless until they find their rest in You."

Jesus is not just a supremely good man. He is the true man, the real man, the proper man. He shows us what we are made to be and in fact what life is really about. Think of the incredible claims He made: "I am the Way, the Truth and the Life". "I am with you always" and "Be of good cheer for I have overcome the world" and "He that has seen me has seen the Father." Then there was the impact He made on those he met. We remember how the Roman Centurion, as he watched the crucifixion said: "Truly this man was the son of God." Earlier Pilate sitting in judgement on Jesus spoke probably more truly than he realised: "Behold the man."

We have got to make up our minds about these claims. Either Jesus was a megalomaniac or his claims were true. The choice is ours.

Love Grandad

LIFE IS A GIFT

Dear Peter, I am sure you have heard of the terrible way the Jews were treated during World War 2.

There is a scene from Leon Uris' book, "Exodus", a popular history of the Jewish people, which tells of what life was like for the people in the Jewish Ghetto in Warsaw during the recent war. The book describes the fierce and persistent attempts of the Nazi troops to eliminate the Jewish inhabitants and how time after time the Jews resisted. Then the Germans decided that they would shut off the Ghetto by building a huge brick wall around it and so seal in the inhabitants to starvation and death. However one Jewish father had a plan. He had a small son and he discovered a narrow space in the wall surrounding the Ghetto through which the boy could wriggle and get away from the Ghetto. Naturally the boy was very reluctant to go through and leave his family and friends. But his father took him aside and explained how important it was that he should escape and go through the wall.

At length the boy agreed to go and just before he started to go through the hole in the wall, his father bade him goodbye, and he said to him: "You are to go out into the world and live for us. You are our hope for the future. In you, what you are and what you do, our people will live on. You will carry on our hope, our faith and our life."

There are two thoughts here to think about.

Think of all that we inherit from those who have gone before us. The comfort, the interest and the possibilities that we take for granted. So much of this has come about by the work, the patience and at times the sacrifice of a great multitude of peoples. Think of all the scientists who have done endless research on drugs that have brought healing and comfort to millions of sufferers. Think of the thinkers, inventors, artists, writers, poets and statesmen and the amazing heritage they have left behind for us to enjoy.

Nor can we forget our parents, relations, friends and teachers who have inspired and encouraged us on our journey. I like to think of it as a great relay race and remember what has been handed on to us as we set out to run our distance.

Belfast city's motto reads: "How much can we return for what is given to us." We can be givers or takers. When we come to the end of our distance what will we be remembered for?

There is a short piece in the Letter to the Hebrews that has always appealed to me, because it indicates that the writer knew about athletics. In fact he may well have been to the Olympic Games. The writer reminds us that those who have gone before us 'surround us, support us and encourage us'. They expect great things of us. Let us be worthy of them.

"And what of our selves? With all those witnesses to faith around us like a cloud, we must throw off every encumbrance, every sin to which we cling, and run with resolution the race for which we are entered, our eyes fixed on Jesus, on whom faith depends from start to finish."

Love Grandad

ON SITTING ON THE FENCE

Dear Peter, This is an encounter I will never forget.

It was 1944 in Germany and I was in a prisoner of war camp about fifteen miles from Dresden. The German authorities had accepted me as a chaplain and enabled me to visit prison camps in and around the city. I was always escorted by an armed German soldier. On the many trips to different camps, or 'kommandos', as they were called, I was accompanied by a great variety of soldiers from all over the Third Reich. The short journeys we had to make on local trains were inevitably very slow with frequent delays, so I had plenty of time to get to know my escort.

I will never forget one such soldier I met. He was a veteran of many campaigns including Russia where he had been seriously wounded. Like most of the many others I met, he was just longing for it to finish and get back to his home and family. As we travelled along we were having a general conversation about the war.

Then suddenly he got to his feet, closed the window, pulled down the corridor blinds with a hasty glance up and down the passage to make sure there was no one about.

I could see that he was quite upset, as he came and sat very close to me and began to talk about the war and how disillusioned he was and he knew that the massive Soviet army had broken across the Eastern frontier and the Allies were also moving on the Western Front. Suddenly he paused again, had another quick look at the passage to make sure that we were alone. Next, with a dramatic gesture he removed his cap and holding it in his hand pointed out the German Eagle, the insignia of the German Army. Then he slowly removed the badge from his cap and reversed it and there on the reverse side were the Hammer and Sickle, the insignia of the Soviet Army.

He paused and very knowingly said ' You see I am ready for what ever wind blows!' Since then I have often wondered what happened to him, when a few months later the Russian Army did arrive. I am sure he was ready for them and did survive!

Of course that was a very unusual situation but it does raise the question how are we to live and make our choices. Will we sit on the fence and wait for things to happen? Will we leave choices and decisions to others and be content to follow the crowd and the easy way? Will we be content to be passive spectators? It is amusing to be in a crowd at a big match and listen to many of them safe in the grand stand keep on shouting advice and sometimes abuse at the players on the field, not forgetting the referee.

It reminds me of the cartoon of the lion tamer inside the cage and having a difficult time with the lion. Round the outside of the cage, in safety, a group of spectators are shouting advise to the tamer and at the same time prodding the lion with their sticks.

Perhaps we should think of this whenever we criticise our local politicians and remember the choices they have to make. It is so easy to refuse to become involved, sit on the sidelines and live in our own personal world. It is easy to avoid political responsibility, the essence of a democratic society. It is easy to ignore sectarianism and inequality in our province. It is easy to forget about the Third World and the millions of people living at starvation level.

Consider the words of John Donne in the 17th century:

No man is an island, entire of itself; every man is a piece of the continent, a part of the main... Any man's death diminishes me, because I am involved in Mankind; and therefore never send to know for whom the bell tolls; it tolls for thee.

Love Grandad

ERIC LIDDELL

Dear Raymond, One of my prize possessions is Eric Liddell's autograph which I got when I met him as a school boy.

I wonder if you have ever seen the film "Chariots of Fire?" It is the story of Eric Liddell who was a student at Edinburgh studying science. He won fame not only in breaking the world record for the 400 metres at the Olympic Games in Paris in July 1924, but also through the circumstances under which he won the race.

However, it was on the rugby field that he first made his mark. This is how the university magazine "The Student" describes him, as a rugby player: "E.H. Liddell (centre three-quarter) has the rare combination, pace and the gift of rugby brains and hands; makes openings, snaps opportunities, gives the 'dummy' to perfection, does the work of three in defence and carries unselfishness almost to a fault."

Small wonder that he was capped for Scotland and played on the team for two years, until he decided to concentrate on his athletics. This is how 'The Scotsman' described the Irish match at Lansdowne Road, Dublin in February 1923: "It was entirely due to a clever move by Liddell that the Scots owed their lead. It was again due to Liddell that Scotland went further ahead... the Edinburgh University player improved on any previous display and he showed that he has now come to appreciate the value of his speed."

In athletics he very quickly made his mark by a series of remarkable victories. For instance in a Triangular International contest with England and Ireland in Stoke-on-Trent, Eric brought victory to Scotland by winning the '100', the '220' and the '440' yards races, something that had never been done before. These and many other remarkable victories opened the way for his supreme sporting triumph at the Olympic Games at Columbus Stadium in Paris in July 1924.

The only question was the distance at which he would run. The 100 metres is regarded as the 'Blue Ribbon' of the Games; It was Eric's great distance and he was the British Record Holder for this distance. For that he would have appeared to be an obvious choice. There was no doubt that his heart was set on it. In the course of the year, however, the lists were published and it was evident that the heats for the 100 metres would be run on Sunday. The British amateur Athletic author-ities did all they could to get the arrangements changed. They knew where Eric stood. When the first announcement had been made, he said quietly but firmly, "I'm not running." That decision, and there could be no hope of changing it, was based on his deeply held principles from which he never deviated.

So he decided that he would concentrate on the 400 Metres Race.

In the heats the world's record was beaten twice in forty-eight hours. In the semi-final he gave evidence of his great reserves, as he won through to the final. This is how another athlete, H. M. Abbrahams, the British Captain, described it. "Drawn on the outside position, Liddell ran from start to finish with an inspired and passionate intensity which gave him a decisive victory in the world record time of 47.6 seconds."

The 'Bulletin' described it as "the crowning distinction of Liddell's great career on the track and no more modest or unaffected world champion could be desired. Liddell has built his success by hard work and perseverance... he received a great ovation from the crowds."

Liddell himself later described an incident that took place just before the race. As he was waiting for the start, a man came up and slipped something into his hand. It was a piece of paper and on it were written these words of scripture, "Them that honour Me I will honour." 1 Samuel 2:30.

A mass of tributes were written and spoken about him but this one from the university magazine "The Student" said it all: "Success in athletics sufficient to turn the head of any ordinary man, has left Liddell absolutely unspoilt, and his modesty is entirely genuine and unaffected. He has taken his triumphs in his stride, as it were, and has never made any sort of fuss. What he has thought it right to do, that he has done, looking neither to the right hand or to the left, and yielding not one jot or tittle of principle either to court applause or to placate criticism. Courteous and affable, he is entirely free from 'gush'. Devoted to his principles, he is without a touch of 'Pharisaism.' The best that can be said of any student is that he left the fame of his university fairer than he found it..."

The story of Eric Liddell speaks for itself. From Edinburgh he went to China as a missionary and worked in Tiensin teaching and preaching. Then when the war came he was interned in a Japanese camp in Weihsien where he died in May 1945.

His whole life was just a study in commitment in whatever he did: in his academic work, his rugby, his athletics, in the use of all his gifts and all his relationships. In all these things he followed the call of Christ to "seek first the Kingdom of God and His righteousness and all these things shall be added unto you."

"Probably the most illustrious type of muscular Christianity ever known," was the verdict of the Glasgow Evening News.

Love Grandad

IS THERE LAUGHTER IN HEAVEN?

Dear Raymond, This must be one of the greatest gifts we can have - laughter.

I am absolutely sure that God has a marvellous sense of humour. I like the way C.S. Lewis puts it: "We are in danger of forgetting that God is not only a comfort but a joy. He is the source of all pleasures; he is fun and laughter and we are meant to enjoy him." Of course it is all very well to say that but what is the evidence?

To start with, humour and laughter are priceless gifts. Who indeed but God could have thought of them? Just think what a marvellous defuser of anger, annoyance, disagreements and embarrassment humour can be. Think of the misunderstandings and the rows that have been avoided by being able to see the funny side.

I vividly remember a very important church meeting, in which there was a deep division of opinion and as a result a hostile atmosphere with feelings running high and voices raised developed. Then one elderly minister got to his feet and told an incredibly funny story about his early life on a farm. I'm not sure how much relevance it had to the furious debate that was going on, but it made everyone roar with laughter. Immediately the atmosphere completely changed and people became relaxed and ready to listen to what others had to say. I am sure we all have had similar experiences. Laughter keeps us from taking ourselves too seriously and helps us to see things in proportion.

Again I sometimes think of the world God has created. Surely he must have had a smile on his face when he made the different occupants of Noah's ark. Think of the incredible shapes and sizes, the inimitable antics and the amazing sounds that come from donkeys, ducks, cats, dogs, chickens, turkeys, monkeys, giraffes, elephants - to mention only a few. Yes - in the beginning God made laughter.

What about Jesus? Surely he must often have had a smile on his face. Children were drawn to him and crowded round him so much that his disciples wanted to chase them away. He very often talked about joy and happiness and I can't imagine he did it with a glum face. It is interesting to remember that the word joy is used over 100 times in the New Testament.

Just think of some of the things he said. One day he was talking about a rich man who was probably very large and "prosperous", as we say in our country. He said that it would be easier for a camel to go through the eye of a needle than for a rich man to enter the Kingdom of God. It was a very serious thing to say but as he thought of the camel and the needle there must have been a smile on his face.

Then he told of the father with a very large family going to bed. The whole family slept together on the one bed. You can imagine all the fuss and talk trying to get them all settled down to sleep. Then at long last they are quiet and at peace. Suddenly there is a great clatter and hammering at the door. At first the father tries to ignore it but then it gets worse and worse until, finally he wearily gets up out of bed and opens the door. I cannot imagine this being told without smiles and laughter.

But the funniest incident was about the man who complained about the mote in his neighbour's eye while he had a plank in his own. Can't you hear the laughter of the bystanders?

Humour is one of God's greatest gifts to us. It is a marvellous antiseptic to pride, conceit and enmity. It is an oil that can lubricate all our relationships and ease the pressure in hard times. It multiplies goodwill, harmony and trust. Its source is in one who wants us to enjoy ourselves to the full and came "to bring life and far more than before."

Love Grandad

LET A MAN EXAMINE HIMSELF

Dear Raymond, Sorry to talk about exams but it is part of the story.
This quotation from Saint Paul always reminds me of examination days, usually in the early summer.

It was a very special atmosphere -the pressure of those last days before hand, reading up the notes, trying to spot likely questions and to memorise useful quotations and key points.

There was one occasion when our examiners did catch us out. It was towards the end of my first year at Queen's University and the subject was Logic.

You may guess our surprise when we went into the examination hall and sat expectantly for the papers to be distributed and Professor Macbeath announced that there were no examination papers, as we were to set our own questions.

At first there was a buzz of surprise and all around there were smiling faces and eagerly each student set about rapidly recording those questions they had just been reading up and were still fresh in their minds. It was not as easy as you might think, as we were to learn.

Eagerly each one of us had scribbled down the question that came most readily to mind. But as the later stages came many of us were busy re-writing the questions in an attempt to cover what we had actually written, as we painfully came to understand how limited our knowledge was!

Why do we have to undergo examinations? I suppose they seem to be the only way of measuring how much knowledge we have and whether we are fit to move on to a further stage in our education.

But I am sure that when Paul wrote out this advice his mind had a much broader and deeper question to ask. He was not just referring to our cleverness or academic knowledge Rather he was asking what sort of a person you are and I am; what we want to do with our lives and our ambitions.

Consider some of the real questions we can ask ourselves. What is my aim in life? What are the things I really care about? What are the things I think most about and dream about?

In one of his last parables Jesus is really talking about examinations, indeed - we could say our 'Finals'. All the nations are gathered together and the test is about how they have treated others.

Had they given food to the hungry, drink to the thirsty, welcome to the stranger, clothes to the naked? Had they visited the sick and those in prison? Then he added this shattering thought: 'For as often as you did it unto one of these you did it unto me'. The Spanish mystic St John

of the Cross sums it up for us:
  'At the end of life we shall be examined on love!'

Love Grandad

PRICE VERSUS VALUE

Dear Raymond, Your Dad will remember the time when, as a small boy, he would study the price list of every Dinky car.

Oscar Wilde once described one of his acquaintances as 'a man who knew the price of everything and the value of nothing'. The times in which we live concentrate very much on the former. Take many of the current phrases 'market forces', the price of the pound and the dollar and mark. Remember also the vast amount of money and energy as well as ingenuity that is devoted to the advertising industry. As I watch the subtlety and skill of the adverts on TV, especially in the run up to Christmas, I am reminded of what Aldous Huxley described as 'subliminal advertising', as the images and actions rush across the screen. It so often seems to be the art of persuading people to buy articles they don't want or need. Are we as aware as we ought to be of the potential of the media both for good and evil?

Of course we are all part of the material and physical world. We have to work, live and look after our bodily needs. But the danger is when exploitation takes place, the other parts of life such as the aesthetic, moral and spiritual are marginalised and neglected. Jesus did acknowledge the physical side of life. Much of his time was spent at a carpenter's bench. He said that 'man shall not live by bread alone' thus acknowledging its importance, but then he goes on to put man's life in a vastly greater perspective and one that is infinitely challenging. His constant theme was the Kingdom of God - the Rule of God.

If you have ever seen the spectacular film "Lawrence of Arabia" you will know that before the first World War, Palestine was part of the Turkish Empire and the Turks were allies of the Germans. General Allenby was commander of the British Forces whose task it was to drive the Turks out of the country and capture Jerusalem the key to the whole country.

A crucial point in the campaign arrived when Allenby's forces had encircled Jerusalem. However it was stoutly defended by the Turks who were very securely established in their defensive positions and it seemed that a very long and costly campaign lay ahead, if the city was to be captured.

A large part of Allenby's forces were dug in close to the Turkish defences on the city wall. Very early one morning the sergeant in charge of the officers' mess decided that he would go and find some eggs for breakfast, so he set out up the road to look for chickens. A short distance along the road he turned a sharp corner and to his horror saw a group of Turkish soldiers running towards him. It was too late to turn back and so he had to stay where he was. But as they approached him the sergeant was utterly amazed to see that they showed no hostility to him and carried no weapons. Indeed they came up to him and treated him with great respect.

When they had stopped in front of him one of them came forward carrying something that seemed quite large and heavy. As he came closer the sergeant saw that he was carrying a very large key. He came forward very solemnly and offered to give it to him. Then he went on to explain that they had come out to surrender and give him the key to Jerusalem.

The sergeant, however, was not impressed and brushed aside the offer of the key and impatiently said: "I don't want your key, I want eggs for the officers' mess." So in dismay the Turks turned and went back to the walls and inside the gate and so a great chance was lost. The sergeant was so wrapped up in the value of the eggs for the mess that he could not grasp the worth and meaning of the key.

Love Grandad

THE ADVENTURE OF LIFE

Dear Raymond, I am sure that our attitude to life is all important, It is fascinating to consider the variety of descriptions that have been use to explain what living means. Every poet and scholar has tried to coin a suitable phrase.

Many have been pessimistic and cynical, others trite and superficial and a few have been positive and hopeful. I've thought a lot about this and decided that for me the most apt is just "The Adventure of Living". I must acknowledge that I owe it to Paul Tournier who wrote a book with this title. I will leave you to decide whether it appeals to you or not.

I came to this decision at a very memorable time in my life. It was the day after I became a prisoner of war when most unexpectedly the naval port of Tobruk on the North African coast was captured by Field Marshall Rommell's Afrika Korps in June 1942. Some 30,000 Allied soldiers became prisoners within 24 hours when the Germans broke through the great perimeter defence.

I can still recall the feelings of dejection and surprise all around. We had been prepared for a battle or evacuation by ship from the harbour, but somehow we never considered the possibility of capture. We spent two unforgettably miserable days in a vast barbed-wire compound out in the middle of the desert. The heat was fierce and our only refuge was a small bivvy tent. Both water and food were very limited. But those days passed and I remember starting to think that this was a unique experience for me. It was indeed an adventure. Hitherto I realised that I had led a very secure and comfortable life with few pressures. Now this as a new challenge a test. It was that sense of being part of a real adventure that stayed with me and indeed sustained me in the darkest hours of the three years that lay ahead. Indeed, I can say they moulded my outlook and encouraged me in many difficult ordeals long since that first experience.

Adventure is a very open word, because we can have so many different kinds - some positive and others negative. It comes to us in so many different ways. Some discover it in sport, or music or drama, others in mountaineering and sailing. Many are happy to use all their energy in their careers. On the negative side, drugs, violence, gambling and pornography are the attractions. It is your responsibility and mine, and this is the heart of what it means to be a real person, to choose where and when we will find our adventure.

But we can go from there and say that God Himself is the supreme adventurer. Of course, I use the word in its most positive sense. I think of the awesome wonder of the universe, its vast space, its multitudes of constellations, mostly undiscovered. Nor can words describe all the limitless variety of animals, birds, trees and plants many of which are as yet unknown to man.

Then, added to all this, is God's supreme adventure in the creation of man. Why did He do this? Because as the Bible says again and again, God is love and he really loves the world He has made. The reason why He has made us is that we can reply to His incredible adventure and do our part to make the whole world a true family held together by His love. That is His great adventure but it is a risky business, because love is always free. It cannot be forced and we have to make our choice.

Love Grandad

SELF CONCEIT VERSUS SELF RESPECT

Dear Raymond, I am sure you know as well as I do what this means.

I once heard of an old Scottish weaver who used to pray: "O Lord help me to hold a high opinion of myself".

I wondered was this self-conceit or self-respect? Because there is all the difference in the world between the two. Indeed whenever we think about it, we can see that self-conceit is the father and mother of all that is wrong with us and our world.

Self-conceit is pride and the primary sin of Adam and Eve in the Garden. It was their desire to be as God themselves. Someone has called it "Man's Godalmightiness".

We all know that this is our basic problem, the desire to do "our own thing". Or as Christopher Robin put it: "There's no one else in the world today and the world was made for me". This is the great temptation to which we have all given in to, to make ourselves the centre of the universe, caring little for others, but seeing things from our own selfish point of view. It was very bluntly put by someone who said of one of his acquaintances; "Gordon is a self made man who worships his creator".

What then about self-respect?

One of the most dramatic situations I was ever in was in war-time Dresden in Germany. It was the spring of 1944 and I was a YMCA Worker and a prisoner of war. I was permitted to visit prison-camps of Allied soldiers but always accompanied by an armed escort.

As we left the Central Station we found that the streets were crowded with people going to work.

Then suddenly, as we made our way along the pavement, people all round us stopped and began to stare at something that was going on in the street. It turned out to be a large group of marching soldiers in fact. But as I looked, I could see that they were not German but British prisoners of war. They had to march a considerable distance, as they were working at the Central Railway Station which was some kilometres from their camp.

Small wonder the people stopped and stared, as they marched past all in perfect step, heads held high, arms swinging, uniforms immaculate, boots perfectly polished and brass buttons gleaming in the morning sun and above all they whistled in unison, as they marched. Small wonder that the people stared in disbelief, as each day the German radio was describing how England was down and out and ready to surrender. As a result the people could hardly believe what they saw and heard.

The secret was the self-respect those men had. They believed in what they had done, though it was to cost them three, four, or five years in prison camps, far from home and family.

Some had come from farms, others from factories and offices, others from the professions. But they had all given up their homes and jobs because they believed that they had to do "their bit", if their country and indeed the whole of Europe was to be saved from the horror of Hitlerism with all the terrible system of mass deportation, concentration camps and gas chambers.

This was the basis of their self-respect. So they were willing to give themselves, precious years of their youth and the misery of prison life, so that those at home and elsewhere could live in freedom and without fear.

Of course self-respect stretches far beyond such grim war-time situations. It is about all of life and it forces us to ask ourselves just who we are and what we are here for. There are some very pessimistic answers to this ultimate question. It was Bertram Russell who once described man "As an accident in a backwater" or "a chance collocation of atoms."

Yet the old Scottish Weaver was right when he prayed, "O Lord help me to hold a high opinion of myself," because he realised who he was and what he was for. If you read the 8th Psalm you will find a marvellous description of who we are. After contemplating the heavens and the solar system the Psalmist exclaims: "What is man that thou art mindful of him?

Then he goes on to speak of the dignity and status of man; "For Thou hast made him a little lower than the angels and hast crowned him with glory and honour. Thou hast made him to have dominion over the works of thy hands: Thou hast put all things under his feet."

We cannot but hold a high opinion of ourselves when we really grasp the tremendous affirmations in the Bible. That we are made in the image of God with the ability to share God's life and think His thoughts after Him. With the gift of freedom, able to choose between right and wrong and able to accept God or reject Him.

But we not only remember who we are but what we're for and that we only really begin to live, when we know in the depths of our being that we are made for God. A very ancient poet knew this long ago when he wrote: "As a hart longs for living streams, so longs my soul for Thee, O God. My soul thirsts for God, for the living God."

There is that deep longing in each one of us to love, to give, to serve and to belong. There is that God-shaped blank that is made to be filled.

Love Grandad